MORE TIME

A BRIEF ANTHOLOGY OF INDIE AUTHOR SHORT FICTION

~ ~

EDITED BY R. TIM MORRIS

MORE TIME

EMPIRE STAMP

Empire Stamp trade paperback edition: July 2020
ISBN 978-1-9990728-2-7 [Paperback]
ISBN 978-1-9990728-3-4 [eBook]

CONTENTS

WANTING

by

LIOR TORENBERG

figured we would get together at some vague later time. Maybe when we were both divorced, or in a retirement home. Things were too complicated now, considering that we worked together and were already in serious relationships. But soon, it would all come together. I'd never been more sure of anything in my life, not even of the unfailing repetition of the seasons. Summer comes after spring, Jason is mine.

He's not an unhandsome man. The veins that run severe through his temples bring out the blue of his eyes. Soft rolls of flesh piled above the back of the beltline; the type of man I could cuddle up with. Not someone who would try to get me to go on morning jogs with him. Not like my boyfriend. His name was Dennis, and he was a handsome man, and I knew exactly how I would break up with him. *"I didn't mean to fall in love with someone else,"* I'd say. *"This just doesn't feel right anymore."* He'd be disappointed but not angry. He'd understand. He's always been good like that.

Truly, I didn't mean to fall in love with Jason. It was at the Holiday Party back in December. It was non-denominational as hell, everything just bright white and covered in snowflake decorations, and among all that carefully manufactured inclusivity, our boss used the phrase 'open kimono' in his speech as a metaphor for corporate transparency. "Christ," someone beside me said.

"I know," I looked over. It was Jason. We rolled our eyes in unison, and that was that. Clear as the tidings of a new season: trees bud, birds chirp, my allergies come back. Simple, inexorable truths.

We'd worked together for a while without ever meeting. Different sections of the office: him in Digital Product by the windows, the whole stoic lot of them typing away all day, squinty-eyed as newborns. Needing to be fed regularly; bags of chips and empty cans of diet coke littering their section of the corporate hive. Me, I was over by the bathroom with the rest of the sales teams. I managed the twerps, the darlings. Everyone had to walk past the sales area to go to the bathroom; the music of my day a mix of calls and flushes. Sometimes when the two lined up with each other—"Hello?" *Flush!* "Goodbye."—I would chuckle. When you hate your job, you have to make your own fun.

Jason and I had a few of our own *Hellos* and *Goodbyes* in passing over the years but we'd never really met, so I re-introduced myself. "Hi Nadine," he said, "Jason."

"I know," I said. Did I imagine it, or did he blush then? I didn't know what to say, but that was fine because our boss was still going on about putting our heads down and working hard, collaborating, believing in our mission. All the while, Jason and I kept looking over at each other and smiling, and when the speech was over and everyone raised their glasses for a toast, we clinked our champagne flutes like a promise.

~ ~ ~

I'll admit, I took it personally when he got sick. It was illogical, but I felt like he had taken something away from me. My future. Our future. How could he just go and get cancer? I thought we had an understanding.

I lazed around Dennis' apartment for an entire weekend after I found out, moist-eyed, just opening the fridge and closing it again. He was worried about me. He knew something was wrong, but how could I tell him what it was? I wasn't planning on breaking up with him, but he kept pressing the issue of my sudden change of personality.

"I'm sorry Dennis," I said. "This just doesn't feel right anymore."

He was disappointed but not angry. He understood. I packed my things and left.

I had been living at Dennis' loft in SoHo for a few months now. It was much nicer than my apartment, which was part of the reason I agreed to live with him in the first place. He had an in-unit washer and dryer and an Italian espresso maker that cost more than my rent. I had sublet my apartment for six months so I went to my parents' house on Long Island.

"How long are you staying for?" my dad asked me, not unkindly, as he helped me make up the bed in my childhood bedroom. I told him that I didn't know. That I had broken up with Dennis and didn't want to be alone right now. I felt like I was lying, even though I was telling the truth. I *had* broken up with Dennis, and I really *didn't* want to be alone. The two were just unrelated.

The real truth would have been that I was sick to my stomach and acting out self-destructively because a co-worker I was infatuated with had gotten terminally ill. I couldn't even admit that to myself, let alone begin to reckon with what I would need to do to put myself back together. I figured I'd just unravel for a bit and let the wonky stitch present itself.

Besides, it was really nice to be at my parents' place for a while. Some people turn their kids' bedrooms into offices or guest rooms or weird hobby areas for candle making and meat smoking, but mine was exactly as I had left it. My massive desktop computer; my glow-in-the-dark stars on the ceiling; my young adult romances piled high on the bedside table. It was almost like they knew I'd come back.

~ ~ ~

It pissed me off the way gossip about Jason spread around the office, though. By noon on Monday I knew that he had testicular cancer. That it had been caught late and was spreading rapidly. That he was bed-bound at Bellevue. No one was sure when—or if—he'd be back. I walked by his desk; I knew it would be empty, but it still made my guts jump straight into my throat to see it like that. His laptop was gone but there was a glass of water on his desk, like he had just stepped away for a moment. There was a hoodie thrown over the back of his chair. When no one was looking, I grabbed it and stuffed it into my bag.

After work, I got on the 6 Train going downtown. I took the hoodie out of my bag. It didn't smell like him; it didn't smell like anything at all. I got off the train at

28th Street and walked ten minutes east to Bellevue Hospital. I bought a balloon at the hospital gift shop. It said "Get Well." Not "Get Well Soon," just "Get Well." Like a command, or a wish.

The receptionist was about my age. Her nametag said "Jenne." I asked which room Jason was staying in.

"Friend or family?" she said. I nodded. "Which one?" she said.

"Yeah, friend."

Her voice turned flat as she echoed hospital policy at me: "We don't disclose personal information about our patients to anyone who is not a direct relative. I recommend you get in touch with your friend directly for his room number." She said that she was sorry, but I could tell that she wasn't. I don't remember what I said then, but it was unconvincing. Something along the lines of: "You don't understand. You have to understand. Please understand."

"I'm sorry," she said again, and it struck me that I had no business being there. I said I was sorry, too, and I left the hospital. It was summer but the night was chilly. I put on Jason's hoodie and sat on the bus stop bench out in front. Going back to my parents' house tonight would wreck me in a way that I couldn't put into words, some failure too large and amorphous to consider. I couldn't go back to my place, and I couldn't go back to Dennis'. I was essentially homeless. Worse, Jason was dying. He was only a handful of feet away from me but I couldn't see him. I wasn't his family, and if I were being honest, I wasn't even his friend.

~ ~ ~

Three buses came and went and I still hadn't decided what to do with myself. I considered the idea of spending the night right there on the bench. It wasn't too chilly with Jason's hoodie on. But one night could lead to another and then another, and I'd end up living right here on this bench. I wondered if people actually became homeless because they were heartsick, or if I was just being melodramatic.

Another bus came and went. I sighed and took out my phone, started looking for cheap hotels near work so I wouldn't have to go back to my parents' place. A woman walked past me; I nearly missed her. It was Jason's girlfriend. I'd seen her at the office a few times. I think he called her "Jo." Thin frame like a ballerina's, a pug-like quality about her, like a rotten smell had forced her features to squish together tightly in the center of her face. I waited until she was a few more feet away before getting up and following her inside.

I walked right past reception, keeping my eyes down, and followed Jo into an elevator. If she recognized me, she didn't say anything. The elevator stopped on the fourth floor, the cancer ward. It was significantly quieter than the lobby. Visiting hours were almost over. Just a smattering of employees littering the hallway: doctors and nurses as flat-affected as Jenne at the front desk had been. I wondered how long you have to work at a hospital before you perfect that face, or if it's something you have to be born with, a prerequisite of sorts.

Jo made a right and then another and ducked into room 403. I found an empty chair down the hallway and waited.

~ ~ ~

I woke up. Someone was tapping me on the shoulder.

"Nadine?" Jason said. He was wearing gray sweatpants and a college t-shirt. He didn't look good. He was pale and thinner than I remembered him, and a bit unsteady on his feet. Jo was standing beside him. He introduced us. Turns out her full name was Josie, which was not a full name at all but just another nickname.

"I knew I recognized you," she said, "Didn't I, Jason? Didn't I say that was your co-worker?" I rubbed the sleep from my eyes and managed a hello, abashed. I really had no business being here. Josie said goodbye to us. She gave Jason a hug and a kiss on the cheek and said she'd be by after work tomorrow.

"You don't have to," he said. She waved his words off and left. Jason turned towards me. It was just the two of us now. It was overwhelming, to have all his attention. "You hungry?" he said. I nodded. "Great, I'm starving."

~ ~ ~

We passed the front desk on the way to the cafeteria. I met Jenne's gaze and smiled. She didn't smile back, but I didn't care. I was getting dinner with Jason.

The hospital cafeteria was mostly empty. A few familial clumps sat scattered throughout the dining area, a handful of loners were eating with headphones on, some so exhausted-looking I couldn't tell if they were visitors or patients. A hospital cafeteria isn't a cheerful place to eat in any situation, but there was nowhere I'd rather have been.

Jason got cream of broccoli soup and a slice of chocolate cake, and I got a hot dog and a diet Coke. We took our trays to a table in a quiet corner of the dining area. He ate eagerly, alternating bites of cake and soup. A dribble of green landed on his chin and stayed. "You know," he said, "I never let myself eat dessert until recently. But my appetite has been so off-and-on lately that I've been eating chocolate cake whenever I can. It's not the worst thing, being medically underweight." He offered me a bite. I shook my head. I hadn't even started on my hot dog. Why had I gotten a hot dog? I picked it up and took a tentative bite out of a corner. "I just wish they let us have beer here," he said. "What damage could it do? I mean, I'm not kidding. It's like insult to injury. I feel like a child here."

"I can bring you beer," I said. He considered me.

"I have to ask, why are you here?" he said, "Don't take that the wrong way. I'm happy you're here. But even my team at work . . . not a lot of people have been visiting me. I think I bum them out."

"You don't bum *me* out," I said. I wanted to reach across the table and grab his hands. I wanted to wipe the soup off his chin.

"Only Jo visits me, and the way she looks at me . . . she looks at me like I'm sick. And I *am* sick, but I don't want to be thinking about that all the time." He chuckled. "I wonder what she'd say if I asked her to sneak me beer." He closed his eyes and pressed his thumb and forefinger into the bridge of his nose. I asked him if he was okay and he said that he was just fine.

"I was having really bad headaches a few weeks ago so I checked myself in. Seems like the cancer is stage four now. I got surgery but it's aggressive; they're thinking that it's already spread to my brain."

"That doesn't sound just fine."

"I guess it doesn't," he said. He smiled weakly; he looked exhausted.

"Oh my god," I said. I took his hoodie off and pushed it across the table. I had completely forgotten that I was still wearing it. "I got cold on the way here so I put it on. You must think I'm the biggest weirdo." He picked up the hoodie and looked at it. "I brought you this. From the office. It's yours."

"It's not mine."

"It was on your desk."

"So they're using my chair as a coat rack. Good to know." He laughed, but the effort didn't quite reach his eyes.

"I'm sorry, Jason," I said. I felt bad for him. I felt bad for myself, too. This was supposed to be my moment of connection. I would give him his hoodie and he would thank me and look me in the eye and tell me that he would be out of the hospital any day now and . . . and . . .

He pulled on the hoodie on top of his sweatshirt. "You stole it for me, so I love it. Fuck 'em," he said. He could tell I was disappointed somehow. He was trying to cheer me up. What a good guy, I thought. I had made the right decision, falling for him.

"I'm thinking of quitting," I said, wondering even as the words came out of my mouth if they were true. They felt true. He said that I *should* quit, that I was underutilized and underappreciated. "How do you know?" I said. I could feel my cheeks flush.

"You've been a sales manager for, what, three years now? And they keep hiring upper management from outside? You're good at what you do. But you're not advocating for yourself, and no one is doing it for you. That's crap."

"How do you know so much about me?" I said.

"Why are you here to see me?" he said. I ate the rest of my hot dog in one big bite, buying for time, but I had misjudged: it was too much food. I covered my mouth with a hand and motioned that I would need a minute. He took a long inhale, a longer exhale. "Anyway," he said, "I'm glad you came. I love my new hoodie. Thanks, Nadine."

Visiting hours were over. I walked him to the elevator and when we hugged goodbye, I realized that it was the first time we had ever touched. "I'll bring you beers," I said as the elevator doors closed. If he answered, I didn't hear it.

~ ~ ~

Jason died a few days later. I was in the office kitchen getting a cup of coffee. Carlos from Human Resources sidled up to me and asked if I could give him a sympathy read on an email. The subject line read: *"Bereavement Announcement. It is with great sadness that we inform you . . ."*

I put my full cup of coffee in the sink and went straight home, called in sick for the rest of the day. My mom was concerned when I called in sick the next day, and the next. I didn't even have the energy to get up to open and close the fridge. She came and sat on the edge of my bed and kissed my forehead like she used to when she was checking for a fever. "I'm sure Dennis will take you back," she said. It took me a moment to even understand who she was talking about.

Had I really not thought about Dennis once since our break up? Had our relationship really meant nothing to me? Two whole years. And yet, I had been at my job for three and it meant even less. It was as if I'd been carried along by some great anaesthetizing wave since I graduated college a decade ago, and the only thing I had truly wanted during that time was Jason. And now, what did I want? My mom brought me a bowl of macaroni and cheese and a glass of water with three ice cubes in it, just like she used to when I was a kid, and that, too, meant nothing to me.

~ ~ ~

Jason's wake was in a small church in Park Slope, Brooklyn on a Saturday. A lot of people from work were there, the same people who didn't visit him when he was in the hospital. Jo was standing with Jason's family by the door, greeting people as they entered. She looked like she belonged with them. His mom looked a bit pug-like, too, but her face could have just been puffy from crying. I hadn't cried yet. How do you mourn the loss of something you never had to begin with? How do you get closure for something that never happened?

Everything was all wrong. I couldn't hear the priest from the back pews and my co-workers were all on their phones, checking email and playing sudoku. The church didn't even look like a church. No stained glass or dramatic apse. It looked more like a high school gym. Half of us were sitting in folding chairs. Everything was all wrong and yet how could it not be? Jason was dead and today had no choice but to be ersatz, ill-fitting as the dress I had borrowed from my mom for the occasion. Tomorrow showed no evidence of being any different.

And what did I want? Right now, I didn't want to be at this wake. I didn't feel Jason here. All I felt was the desire to cry and get some sort of relief from this unbearable inertia, this sourceless heartbreak.

I got up and left, walked out the door of the church and into the summer air, went down one block and then another and started picking up my pace, walking faster and faster until I was running, feet flying in long strides, elbows pumping, shoes slapping the ground like the beginnings of a round of applause, like a chant emitted upwards from the concrete itself, each utterance louder than the one that came before. I want, I want, I want.

I turned a corner and saw a group of kids clustered in the middle of the block. They looked to be about twelve or thirteen, mostly boys. The largest of the group had a wrench clasped in both hands and was trying to open a fire hydrant. I stopped running. He yanked on the wrench, the tendons of his neck taut and glinting with sweat, his arms straining. He pulled again. He pulled.

A gush of water surged forward and upward, a shimmering translucence that arced from one side of the street to the other. The kids whooped and hollered and ran out into the stream. It was the greatest thing I'd ever seen. I was breathing hard from running. The air tasted like summer: magnolia and honeysuckle from the flower shop down the block, suntan lotion, linens hung to dry on balconies. I swallowed it in gulps. I wanted to join them, so I did. I walked into the water and the cold, jetting flow hit my body like a comfort, a consolation. I began to cry in violent shudders, just standing there with my mouth open and my eyes closed and weeping. I began to wonder what I must look like, then realized that I didn't care. I listened for the sound of sirens, but there was only city noise, bird song. Just the rush of the deluge and the heat of the concrete and the sun overhead, bearing witness.

IN MYSTERIOUS WAYS

by
ZEV GOOD

The man jumped from the top floor of the Westin's parking deck downtown just after two o'clock on Tuesday afternoon. He hadn't considered this in the weeks before, but had he done it earlier or later in the day, there would have been more people on the sidewalk and someone else might have been crushed. As it turned out, he was the only casualty.

Later, at six and eleven, it would be on the news and people—none of them actual witnesses—would be perplexed. They would say they hadn't known this man, or why he did it. They would wonder aloud why, their eyes wide from the shock of this thing they hadn't seen. They would look into the camera and say what a terrible thing it was for a man to jump to his death from the top of a parking deck. One of them would wonder *What if a child had seen?* On TV, it is always good to mention the potential devastating effects an incident might have on a child. Those responsible for the news believed this was important, as it created interest. No one bothered to consider the foolishness of it, because there were no children present when the man jumped.

There were two witnesses: a young woman from Mexico with the name of a famous American singer, and a black man with a Spanish name. The man hit the sidewalk between them. In the second after it happened, they looked first at this thing that had made such a noise when it fell from the sky and saw that it was a man—or, rather, what remained of a man—the blood already pooling around him and seeping from his mouth, his nostrils, and his wide-open eyes, which were green; then they looked at each other, one's shock evident to the other. Her name was Diana. His was Alfredo.

The black man, who was tall and quick and did not think, leaped over the crushed body, put himself between the woman and the dead man, said, "It's okay. Don't look. Just don't look."

She looked anyway and saw, just as her vision blurred and she felt herself passing out in the arms of this man whose name she would never know, something gather in the air above the crushed corpse: the man's soul, or his ghost, his *fantasma*. Around her, people screamed as they realized what had happened. Diana did not scream. She was not afraid. She knew about death.

When she was five, her father, in a rage, shot and killed her mother. He believed Diana's mother was sleeping with a man named Fernando. Diana's father was waiting when her mother came home from somewhere. He yelled at her and she yelled back and he shot her with a gun he had bought just three days earlier. Then, sobbing and frantic, he aimed the pistol into his mouth and pulled the trigger. Diana found them, her father's body having fallen across her mother's, their blood mingling and spreading beneath them. Diana was terrified and confused, but she ran the five kilometers to the house of her *tía*, screaming that someone had killed her mother and father. When she was older she understood that her father was the killer. No one told her outright, but she knew from the things they said. This was how she learned about death.

"Sit here. It's okay." The black man led her to a bench where, before the man jumped to his death, people waited for the bus. Those people were on their feet now, asking what happened and craning their necks to see.

Diana wondered if they, too, had seen when the man's soul leave his body there on the sidewalk. She wouldn't look again. She knew the soul or ghost or whatever was gone now. These people wanted to see the body, the blood, not the man's spirit. When the bus came a few moments later, she boarded it and sat in the back where she could not see the body or the crowd of people gathering around it. That night, she would dream she was standing outside the hotel where she had applied for a job as a housekeeper, and that as she waited to cross the street, a young man with green eyes and a yellow tie would step alongside her. She would smile and he would smile, and Diana would know that he was better where he was now.

~ ~ ~

When the police arrived, and after them the news teams, Alfredo told them there had been a woman. "She was standing with me when he fell," he told them, but that woman was nowhere to be seen, so they did not care about her. They asked him what he had seen, how it had happened, and he told them. He had shaved that morning with a dull razor and he scratched his chin as he spoke, first to the officers and then to the reporter, who was Asian and wore perfume. "I was just standing there, and he fell. Just like that. WHUMP! You know?" He felt the need to make it clear he had nothing to do with it. "I didn't know him and I don't know why he did it." The pretty Asian reporter asked what he'd thought when it happened and Alfredo said that he was just glad no children had seen it. This will be on the news later, Alfredo scratching his chin and saying this.

He would worry for weeks about why, of all the people who could have been standing on the sidewalk when this man he will never know jumped from the parking deck, it had to be him. People he knew said the Lord tested people and he guessed this was a test, because he wasn't supposed to be there at that time, on Tuesday afternoon. He should have been working, but he had quit his job over the weekend. He was tired of washing dishes for a living. He had decided he was too old to wash dishes. He would find something else to do that paid more and was not so demeaning.

His ex-wife would be furious. She would want the child support. Already she wanted more than he could pay and she was always threatening him: she would take him to court, she would not let him see the kids, she would call her brothers and they would deal with him. He would remind her that she was the one who told him to find something else, that a forty-four-year-old man should do more than wash dishes, that he should be ashamed of himself. He would tell her that, but she would still be angry.

"The good Lord works in mysterious ways," Alfredo's mother, who was very pious, would say. "He wants you to learn something from washing dishes." She was not ashamed of him.

"What He want me to learn, then?" Alfredo asked. He was not as devout as his mother.

"That's between you and Him."

Alfredo guessed he had learned all he needed: that a man his age with three grown children by one woman and two more by the woman who now hated him so needed a better job. He wasn't sure what this other thing meant. What was to be learned witnessing a man half his age jumping to his death?

"Everything happens for a reason." His mother said this a lot, but Alfredo was not so sure. He could find no sense in it. He sat in his apartment—a motel room, really; he rented by the week—that night after watching himself on the news and wondered if he'd imagined the young woman. He was drinking beer he couldn't afford and his neck and chin still itched from that dull razor, and he wondered if he'd imagined her. He could remember the face of the dead man: he'd had green eyes and black hair and his tie was yellow. Alfredo remembered how the blood came out of his eyes and nostrils and mouth, like a slow-motion replay on TV. But he could remember nothing about the young woman, as if she hadn't been there at all.

~ ~ ~

Diana told no one. She didn't want to talk about it because she wasn't sure how to say that she'd watched a man die, then his soul leave his body. She didn't want people to think she was crazy. She did not watch the news. She didn't want to be reminded. She knew enough about death.

Four months ago, she used all the money she had saved, and planned to send her *tía*, to get an abortion. She didn't need another child. Her boyfriend agreed; neither of them needed this responsibility. She had a son and a daughter, living with her aunt in Mexico; he had none and didn't want any. He drove her to the clinic, waited outside in his car, smoking cigarettes and listening to Los Tigres del Norte and talking on his cell phone to another girl, who was younger and prettier than Diana. Afterward, he drove her back to her apartment. They did not speak of what they had done, like in a movie when two people murder someone and bury the body and never discuss it. A week later, when he called to tell her he was seeing someone else, she was not surprised.

In her dreams, that baby was a boy with green eyes and he could fly. *"¡Mirame, mami—puedo volar!"*

"Sí. Te veo."

In that dream, she called him Michael, but she didn't know why. Perhaps, like herself, after a famous American singer.

~ ~ ~

Alfredo found it odd, when he thought about it, that he saw so little of his three grown children. One daughter lived in California where it never got cold. She was the eldest. A son lived in Chicago, which was nothing like California. The other son, the youngest of the three, lived in Atlanta, but Alfredo never saw him. They never spoke on the phone and—this surprised Alfredo—they never passed one another on the street. This son visited Alfredo's mother often, and she was his source of news about this son: he'd graduated high school, he'd graduated college, he was a graphic designer, he was a homosexual.

Alfredo knew where his son worked, and where he lived, but he never called and never visited. He told people that he was ashamed of his gay son; what he never said was that he was more ashamed of himself. What son wanted anything to do with a father who washed dishes for a living and drank beer he couldn't afford, alone in his motel apartment with all the lights off?

When this son was born, Alfredo wanted to name him after himself, but his wife wouldn't hear of it. The child needed his own name, she said, and named him Deon, which Alfredo hadn't liked because it sounded too much like a woman's name. When this son was older, he went to an attorney and changed his name, and now he was William. Alfredo liked that better, even if it wasn't his own name.

After watching the man die on the sidewalk, Alfredo thought he might call his son. Being close to death made people do things like that. It made them want to get closer to the people in their lives because it became clear that anything could happen. Alfredo was worried something might happen, but he wasn't sure what it might be. Still, though, he did not call. He asked his mother and she said that his son was doing just fine.

~ ~ ~

Two days after the man with green eyes jumped to his death, a woman from that hotel called Diana to schedule an interview, and could she come the following Monday at ten a.m.? Diana thanked the woman, whose name she would not remember. She said she would be there on Monday.

She rode the bus, then the train, where she sat beside a man her mother had loved. Diana didn't know this, though he smiled at her and said, *"Hola."* She smiled back and said, *"Hola."* They didn't speak again. The man who had loved her mother spoke in whispers to a young black man who was with him, but they spoke English and Diana didn't understand what they said.

The train stopped. Diana got off and rode the escalator up and walked to the hotel. There was nothing where the man had fallen the week before. It was like it had never happened. No one stopped to point and say, "Here. This is where he fell when he jumped."

She didn't notice, but the young black man and the man her mother had loved had left the train station after her. She walked into the hotel and didn't look back to where they stopped on the sidewalk, first looking up at the dizzying height of the building, then down at the place on the sidewalk, where now there was nothing.

"It was here?" asked the man, whose name was Fernando. He had flown in from Texas to bury his son, who had jumped to his death from the top floor of the parking deck of this famous hotel. He was tired and anguished.

"Yes," said the younger man. His name was William.

Fernando stood silent, his eyes closed. He stood like that for a long time. People walked around him, did not notice the man or his misery. He opened his eyes finally and gave William, who had been his son's lover, a weak smile. "Thank you. We can go now."

They walked back to the train station and rode the escalator down, boarded the next train, and went north. They didn't speak. Later that afternoon, Fernando returned to Texas on a plane full of people who had no idea he had buried his youngest son, Miguel—who preferred, when he was a man, to be called Michael.

He closed his eyes and remembered the face of a woman he had loved years ago who was long dead, thought how very much she had resembled the young woman on the train that morning. And he thought of his son.

When he was little, four years old, Miguel tied a yellow towel around his neck like it was a cape and climbed onto the bed of his father's old pickup truck.

"*¡Mirame, papi—puedo volar!*"

"*Sí. Te veo!*" Fernando had laughed, but even at that height, a tiny boy could hurt himself. "*Pero . . . ten cuidado, hijo.*"

Miguel had laughed. "*¡Voy a volar!*" And he went up on the tips of his toes, spread his arms. The wind caught the towel that was his superhero's cape, and for an instant it was like he was actually flying.

THE PHONE RINGS ONE EVENING

by

EMMA DESHPANDE

Estelle stops singing and waits for the phone to ring out.

It's on a coffee table, just a few steps away from where she's standing by the window. Everything in this apartment is designed to have *easy access*, which Estelle thinks is a nice way to describe condescending architecture. When the living room leads into the kitchen, the bathroom, and the bedroom, how can she have enough wall space for her china plates? She could only bring one cabinet with her when she moved, and all the dishes inside are stacked four or five high. It's precarious. Some of the people in this retirement community, like Ursula from down the hall, hold on to furniture as they move around a room. Estelle never invites people over, and her dishes remain safe.

The voicemail activates, and plays over the speakerphone:

Hi Estelle, it's Paul.

And Lucy. We're wondering where you want to go for our Wednesday dinner? We're up for anything, as always! Call us back when you have a chance. We're about to call Janey, so we'll let you know if she has any suggestions.

Bye!

Bye now!

She wishes she had turned the phone off earlier. Lawrence always unplugged the phone for her, when she took a nap or when she felt stressed. She never wanted him to. How would they know if someone called? There were any number of potential emergencies with her children, her parents, her in-laws. He never apologized. You needed to rest, he said, when she asked why there weren't any messages. The phone would've disturbed you. It was a brave stance in the decades before answering machines.

She understands him more now.

She hasn't rehearsed enough today, so she won't call Paul and Lucy back until tomorrow.

Estelle knows she's a likely candidate for the Easter mass solo. She's known the choir director for longer than some of the other singers have been alive. And wasn't she voted Best Voice when the retirement community organized a superlatives night?

She asked for a copy of the sheet music for Easter service and she sings along every day, to make sure she knows every note. She has four more days to practice. They'll announce the soloist on Sunday, after morning mass.

When she sings the solo, her voice will be the only one in the church. The music will raise her up to God.

She and Lawrence met at church. By her mid-twenties she was impatient for a husband; most of her friends were married or engaged. On Sundays she scanned the crowd for any bachelors, any men who seemed single and interested in her. And one Sunday, during the prayer after communion, she saw him.

Estelle always waited several seconds for the congregation to be engrossed in their prayers before she lifted her head. How was she supposed to know how serious a man was about religion unless she saw him at prayer? That day, a young man on the other side of the aisle stared straight ahead. He must have sensed her watching, because he looked over and smiled. She blushed and looked back down. When prayer ended and everyone sat back in their seats, she lingered at the bench to ask forgiveness for her boldness. Never again would she take time away from prayer to look at men.

After the service, she waited in line to congratulate the priest on his homily. Lawrence joined the line behind her and introduced himself. I couldn't concentrate on the service with a woman like you in the room, he told her. You're perfect. Estelle thought that he was perfect, too. They were roused from prayer at the same moment, drawn to each other. This was the man she was meant to marry.

But when they were married, Lawrence never wanted to pray with her. Prayer is personal, he said, and you have a better connection to God if you pray to Him alone. He said things like that. Sentences, masqueraded as universal truths, that were only ever addressed to her. He never even spoke to their children like that.

She deferred to him on most things, but she never accepted that prayer was solitary. As a child, she had watched her parents pray together. They had bent their heads over the rosary, coiled around their intertwined fingers, and recited the Our Father, Hail Mary, and Glory Be in whispered unison. They had been overcome by His spirit, overcome together, and Estelle knew her marriage was also bonded by faith.

If Lawrence had a late night at work, she stayed up until he came home. She never said her evening prayers until he said his, even though he went to another room for privacy. She prayed for him while he was in the hospital when she was sure he was praying, too.

It's been a year since he passed away, and she can feel herself drifting. She wishes he had taught her how to pray alone. She hasn't been to confession in months; the penance for every sin is prayer, and without Lawrence, she's forgotten how to speak to God.

When Estelle sings her solo, her voice will be the only one in church and He will have to listen to her. She will feel heard again.

She flips back to the first sheet of music. She'll go over the songs once more before dinner.

~ ~ ~

Paul replaces the phone in its receiver.

Well, Lucy says. I'm sure she'll call us back any minute. She probably wasn't near the phone.

She knows we call this time every Wednesday, he says. Where do I need to go to find dependable people?

He thought all their problems were solved when they moved out of their house into this retirement community. No stairs, showers with seats, and toilets with handles. All the energy spent worrying about Lucy (and increasingly, himself) whenever they weren't in the same room could be put into other projects. He reads more, and he's made notes for an essay he'd like to start writing soon. He'll type it up on the computer. It's difficult to hold a pen for long periods of time these days, so he can't write in a notebook like he used to do. He won't buy a computer for their apartment when there are plenty downstairs in the rec room, free with their rent, but he finds it difficult to concentrate in a room with only one window. The local library might have computers near a window, though. He'll ask when he returns his books next week.

Lucy watches her husband go silent. She'd like to call Janey and hear someone else's voice, even if all they get is another answering machine. Where does he need to go to find dependable people? He didn't say *we*, he said *I*. It was the question of someone alone, alone despite his wife sitting in the chair next to his.

She knows Janey's number by heart. She picks up the receiver and dials, clears her throat to prepare for her *Hello!* Paul will join in when he needs to.

~ ~ ~

Janey doesn't want to go out tonight. She knows she'll talk about Ted again, too much. It's not that people mind. They seem to like her stories. She feels sick after telling them, though. She's safer at home, in front of her computer.

She loves YouTube. She doesn't know how anyone does anything with the lure of millions (billions?) of videos waiting to be watched. It's a good thing she doesn't have to work anymore. And a good thing that her eyes haven't gone yet. She loves to watch, to look at the young people's faces and the decoration of the rooms behind them to figure out what it is that makes them brave enough to create these videos in the first place.

The first video appeared on her recommended list by some benevolent act of the universe. She'd never searched for anything like it. She didn't know such a thing existed. *My coming-out video.* She watched one, and more and more appeared on the right side of her screen. So many people who identified as gay, lesbian, men, women, no gender at all. She watched until two in the morning that first time. Her knees and back ached for a week. She still watches. There are always more videos.

She's mesmerized by them. She wants to meet them, gather them together in a room and look at them all. Speak to them. She's not sure she has the courage to do that. She wants to, one day. She wants to listen to them before she says anything.

She wants to tell Ted about them. Ted would want to meet them. She wouldn't be afraid to speak to them.

I'm Ted and this is Janey, she would say, And we're lesbians. We're in love.

She said that at home sometimes, more often out in the world—when it was safe and when it wasn't. When it was, they were at a bar or a party where they knew everyone liked them. Janey liked to sit at a table in these places and watch people while she drank. She never got over how much she liked seeing people flirt. Smiling, touching hands, dancing so close that Janey would have to look away and press her glass to her cheeks to cool them down. Then a drunken Ted would drag her out to the dance floor, among all those flirting couples, and yell out their love. People didn't always hear. If they did, they would smile or cheer. Then they'd stay on the dance floor and become one of those dancing couples, until neither of them could stand waiting and they went back to their apartment.

Ted always spoke louder when it wasn't safe. They would overhear people talking about men and women getting married, how they were meant for each other, how it was the natural thing to do. Ted would lean over and whisper in Janey's ear: I'm Ted and this is Janey. We're lesbians, and we're in love. Her *Got a problem?* at the end was unspoken, obvious. It was directed at the people they'd overheard, and at Janey. They both knew that Janey had a problem, and had to stifle a reprimand for Ted to be quieter. The first and only time she complained aloud, the pain in Ted's face was too great to be observed. She walked away from Janey and didn't speak to her for the rest of the day.

These young people are in pain, too. People say terrible things in the comments, as awful as what she and Ted used to overhear. Perhaps worse: these words are permanent, available to be read and re-read. Often the young people coming out sound angry, and they cry. Janey cries with them, sometimes so much that she needs to pause the video to collect herself. She wonders how often they watch themselves back. She'd like to make her own video, and watch herself. *My coming out.* The more videos she watches, the more she knows she should make one, too. She doesn't own a camera. None of her friends in this retirement community know how YouTube works, either, and she's afraid the young people who work here will laugh at her if she asks them. Besides, she doesn't want to tell anyone she knows. She wants to tell these people of YouTube, people who only exist from the shoulders up within one corner of their bedrooms.

She hasn't really changed if she can only tell the truth anonymously. But it's something. It's better than disappearing, which is what Ted did.

Fifteen years into the relationship, Ted gave up. I'm tired of this, she told Janey. I'm leaving. It was a Monday: September fourteenth, 1992. Janey remembers that it was warm for September, because she was confused about the coat Ted was wearing. It made sense when she realized Ted was really leaving, and moving far away to a city where no one knew her. Janey doesn't know anything else. Ted might have fallen in love with someone else, she might have never loved again. She doesn't do anything now, because Janey started searching for her almost every day when she got a computer installed in her apartment. A few months ago, she found her first and last result: Ted's obituary. The relative who wrote it was a grand-niece, apparently—the woman's mother, Ted's only niece, had been a teenager when Ted and Janey lived together. It was short, about where Ted went to school and what she did for a living. *Theodora O'Neill passed away yesterday morning, peacefully . . .*

It took a long time for Janey to read the rest. She couldn't stop crying. She wondered if her eyes would go before she had a chance to read it, the one reportage of Ted's life. They didn't. Five weeks after she found it she managed to read the entire paragraph without crying, and she wondered if she was finished mourning.

Janey was angry when Ted left her. She thought the fact of them being together was the most important thing, enough to make up for the fact that they lived in secret. She knows now that it isn't. She talks about Ted at every opportunity—what she liked, what they did together, how they danced. No amount of sympathy from her listeners makes up for the way they respond, which she can never bear to correct: You must miss him very much.

She scrolls down from the video she's just finished watching and reads the comments. There's no one to help her with her video. She doesn't need them. She can do this with words. She clicks on the box labelled Add Public Comment.

I want to thank you, she types, *for doing something I was never able to do. You are very brave. I've been in love with a woman named Theodora since I was twenty-three, and she left me because I couldn't come out as you have. Neither of us could. There were only a few places . . .* She writes about their parties. The way that Ted's whispering in her ear, which should have been loving, became nasty because of their secret. *My name is Janey,* she types. *And I am a lesbian.*

She posts the comment, then closes her browser and turns off her computer. It's too late to meet up with anyone for dinner. She doesn't mind. She's glad she stayed in. She stands up and walks to the kitchen, planning what to cook for herself. Something warm—she has enough vegetables for a stew.

The emails arrive while she cooks and eats, and they continue after she goes to bed. She'll see them in the morning, when she opens YouTube to watch a video after breakfast. She expects people to protest, and they will. She'll also see everyone who liked and replied to her comment with support. They're proud of her. They're glad she shared.

~ ~ ~

Call us back when you have a chance!

Paul doesn't add, Bye, like he usually does.

Janey didn't pick up after three rings, like she usually does, he says.

I don't know what's going on. I don't know why they'd both be busy when we always spend Wednesday evenings together. Lucy's angry now. She's angry that their friends made her husband seem like a stranger, and she's angry because she understands what he meant. They should be dependable. They aren't.

How long do we wait? Paul asks.

I don't want to wait. By now we've always decided on a restaurant and we're figuring out how to get there. I'll be hungry soon. I think we should pick a restaurant ourselves and go.

Without telling them? Paul doesn't remember the last time he felt this excited. They aren't breaking a rule—a rule of courtesy, maybe—and he feels like he's in a film. You know, you're right. Let's just go.

Okay. Where?

Where? Paul repeats. He didn't expect this question. It's easier to come up with a restaurant when four minds are on the task.

What are you in the mood for? she asks.

Paul knows he has to answer, because if he asks Lucy what she's in the mood for, she'll be annoyed that he can't make a decision. Italian, he says. I always like Italian.

So do I. They smile at each other. They're thinking of the same Italian restaurant, the one a block away from their old house where they had dinner every Friday. They knew Tommy, the owner, very well—he usually joined them for a drink after their meal. This is on me, he'd say when the round arrived, Because you both know you're keeping me in business. He passed away before they sold their house, so their last meals at the restaurant were subdued without the promise of seeing him.

Lucy tears up thinking about it. Paul knows why she retrieves the handkerchief stored in her sleeve to blow her nose before she says, Have we been to good Italian restaurants around here?

I can't remember, Paul says, Off the top of my head. Why don't we look it up on the internet? His smartphone, a gift from his oldest daughter and her husband, always stays charging at the desk. They've told him he can carry it around with him. It's a small computer, and he knows that computers stay plugged in or they don't work. He walks over to the desk to unlock it and open the internet.

Oh. Okay, Lucy says. She wishes they didn't need to look up a restaurant. She misses the days when everything was recommended by a real person with an anecdote like, The dessert looked really delicious, and Nora—you've met our daughter, haven't you?—she was a baby at the time and she wouldn't stop fussing, so we had to leave the second we finished our entrées.

Paul believes online reviews are just as good as those anecdotes. Look at this place, he says to his wife. Five stars from nearly everyone. And it's family owned.

Lucy finds it difficult to judge the atmosphere of a place from a photo smaller than her palm. She's too hungry to be particular tonight. That looks great, she says.

I'll call downstairs to get us a taxi, Paul says.

A taxi? How much will that cost?

It doesn't matter, he says. He's already decided not to get an entrée or a dessert to offset the transportation cost. We're too late for the evening shuttle, and it'll be a nice treat. Do you think we'll need to make a reservation?

Not for two people. She doesn't mean to sound annoyed, and she regrets making her husband wince. I mean, they can always make room for two.

~ ~ ~

Two people aren't enough for a conversation. They run out of things to talk about in the taxi. They've spent the entire day together, so they can't ask, What have you been up to? the way they do with Janey and Estelle.

When they arrive at the restaurant, Lucy is sure that they've been there before. Paul doesn't say anything. Has he forgotten? She doesn't want to ask and find out that he has.

Paul wonders why Lucy doesn't point out that they did eat here, right after they moved into the retirement village. She always accompanies these reminders with a detail like, We sat next to that young couple who didn't say a word to each other, the entire meal, because they were both on their phones. It was shocking. Has she forgotten? Does she think he isn't interested in those details anymore? He wishes he could remind her with something that happened that night. He doesn't remember in specifics like she does.

Lucy's right—they don't have to wait for a table. When they sit down, Paul asks, What do we usually talk about? When we're with Estelle and Janey, I mean?

We usually talk about their spouses, Lucy says. She scans the menu. She's worried that her husband's memory is going. She remembers what she ate last time: spaghetti carbonara, and it was strangely salty. She'll stick to a meat dish this time. What if Paul is losing his memory? It's restaurants now. Vacations will be next, then the first apartment they lived in, the house they sold before moving here. Will he forget her name? Will he forget her?

Lucy? Are you alright?

Yes, of course. She blows her nose. Paul reaches across the table and squeezes her hands. The menu must remind her of Tommy's.

Do you know what you'll order?

She clears her throat. I think the chicken. You?

I haven't decided yet.

She nods. Anyway, you were asking what we talk about when we're out with the girls. It's usually about their spouses. They tell stories, and then we tell our stories.

Ah, of course. So we can't really do that without them. Not unless we tell our own stories to each other.

Lucy knows she's supposed to laugh. It's difficult. When Paul's mind goes completely, she'll have to tell their stories to him. She'll do all the talking, which he hates. Will he remember that he hates it, though?

I hope Janey and Estelle are alright, she says. It is strange that they didn't answer us. And they've been doing so well lately. Janey especially. I'm much less worried about her than I was when we met. She used to cry nearly every time she mentioned Ted.

He seems like he was a very special man, Paul says. I wish we could have met him.

Lucy smiles. I'm sure they were lovely to see together. Very devoted.

You know what I think about Estelle? I think we should set her up with someone. Do you know any eligible men?

Eligible men? Lucy laughs. I don't think so. No one where we live seems even remotely appealing to me.

That's because you have everything you could ever need.

Oh, I do?

Yes. He takes her hand and kisses it. She blushes, and he likes that he can still make her blush. Have a look around for men you think might suit Estelle.

I don't know, Paul, she says. Is this a good idea? She's never expressed interest in it.

She wouldn't *express* interest. She'd be afraid that people would think she was a bad widow, even though enough time has passed. She seems lonely, don't you think?

She does seem very bored. Maybe it would be a good idea. Let's start looking tomorrow.

It's a plan.

Lucy likes the idea of being a matchmaker. They could go around the retirement village, setting people up, like those shows on HGTV where a married couple improves other people's homes and lives. They could pretend they're in their own show. What about Janey? she asks. Should we set her up, too?

Oh, no. Not yet. She's in a very different stage of grief.

Paul sounds so serious that she smiles. A different stage of grief? she says. You're so scientific about this. Do you think about it a lot?

Sometimes. Not a lot. He pauses. She can tell that this isn't part of some matchmaking act. I thought that was why we spent so much time with them, he says. To plan a little.

To plan? When she realizes what he means, she's so angry that she can barely speak. Do you mean plan for each other's *deaths*? Is that what you think about? Her vision of telling him stories on the couch of their apartment is replaced by a vision of him sitting at a bar in a suit, calling over every woman who walks past him. And he's successful, of course, because he's always been charming.

Lucy—

How dare he say something like this, when she already felt heartbroken by the thought of him losing his memory? He didn't know why she was delicate. He must have known something was wrong, though. He asked her. And then this.

So, what, you want to be set up the way you're planning to set up Estelle? Lucy says. She shakes her head. I'm sure you're already scanning the village for potential candidates. I can't believe this.

Yes. His voice lowers. I am thinking about it. Not for myself. For you.

For me? Don't be ridiculous. You're not—

Not right now. But you never know—

Don't say that. I won't listen to this.

I couldn't live without you, Lucy, he says. There's no chance. So that's why I look. To prepare myself. Because I'll be watching, and I don't want to be too upset.

Oh, she says. Sometimes—sometimes I feel like I already miss you. Is that terrible?

No, he says. I think it's flattering.

Well. She blows her nose and keeps the handkerchief in her hand. At this rate, she'll need it again in a minute. You should feel very flattered, then.

The waitress interrupts them. Hi, you two. How are you doing this evening?

Lucy wipes her eyes and Paul coughs. I know we don't look it, he says. But we're very well.

Are you ready to order?

I'll have the chicken parmesan, please, Lucy says.

And I'll have the spaghetti carbonara.

Oh, no! She speaks without thinking. Don't get that. It was so salty last time.

He exhales. You do remember coming here before. I was afraid you'd forgotten.

I was afraid *you'd* forgotten. She reaches for his hands. I was so afraid—

He smiles. It's okay. We both remember.

The waitress clears her throat. Do you need more time?

FOXTAIL

by

PERRY WOLFECASTLE

How did I get here?

You want to know what got me here, my experience, to put it all down on this tape? Yeah, I can do that for you. I can do that. From the beginning. From before it all went—no, I am getting ahead. You told me that was bad. I need to start at the start. Before the madness.

Was I mad?

Am I mad?

You say I am mad.

I do not think I am mad.

It was summer, I am sure of that. We had just had the solstice celebrations. I always go home for that. The well dressing is a family tradition for me and mom, we help lay the flowers around the well—lavenders and daffodils with a handful of daisies here and there—it was magical, everyone agreed. The parish council had hired a funfair with a big wheel. Farmer Collins had agreed to let them set the whole thing up in his south fields, the cows had not been allowed to graze down there yet. With the sun shining down on everything that day, I felt more of myself than I had in years. The stresses of the city melted away for a few hours in the scent of popcorn and the honeysuckle wafting in from the next field. I got on the big wheel with my dad and I was a child again, I even had the plaited pigtails to match. Innocent and free twenty feet in the air, the world was good. Limitless.

How I wish I could go back to that day.

The feeling lasted all that weekend and well into my working week. There was a spring in my step as the summer sun burnt away at the smog of the city. Flowers planted at every street corner caused scents to wander into the air. Grime and crime were superseded by light and hope. I had always felt alone in the city. It is hard not to when you live alone in a one bed apartment with only your editor and interviewees to chat to on the daily. My social life was primarily online, and it was really heating up over my pictures of the funfair. Everyone loved them, and in all honesty, I loved the attention they garnered. From the arrangement of flowers, the big wheel, and the beautiful landscape shots I had taken that night, I was popular—for once in my life—I felt like the popular one. My favourite, which also seemed to be gaining likes at a rapid pace, was a selfie of my mother and I, arm in arm, beaming in front of the well.

Then he liked my post.

I did not know how he had seen me, nor did I question it, that's how social media works: people just pop up from anywhere. All I needed to know was that he was as cute as the day was long. That is all it was at first. A like here and there. He would like my well dressing photos and I would like a selfie of his. Those dark eyes and well-maintained beard got me every time; I mean every time. This guy was hot.

He made me feel—and I know this sounds stupid—but he made me feel wanted. As time went on, we would spend hours each day just sending funny GIFs to each other. It was cute, exciting.

Then he private messaged me, and not just with a "hey" but with his phone number. I felt as though my heart would catch fire. This was all I had ever needed in a way I never knew I was missing. Here was a guy who wanted to get to know me—me of all people, sad little lonely me. I had lived in this city now for five years and in that time not made one friend. It is not that I never tried, but as you get older it becomes harder to make friends, to make that transition from acquaintance, you know? Five years of watching people meeting for a morning coffee, seeing groups in suits greeting each other for after work drinks as I walked to and from the office alone. I would see couples out on dates and have a pang of heartache, I wanted to be the one sitting in fancy restaurants laughing and smiling, wine glass in hand. Was this my chance now? I had hoped that in going home for the well dressing I would see old friends and reconnect, maybe see David, my high school boyfriend, again and have some fun. When I caught up with the old gang who were still there in that sleepy village each felt like a stranger to me, and an introduction to David's wife and their new baby left me with a pit in my stomach. I never realized how lonely I had been until that moment; here was the chance of a real human connection. I had retreated into social media, tricking myself into thinking that my online life was all I needed, all I wanted. I know now that I was missing a human touch. I needed to get out from the four walls that felt like a prison, a lifetime of solitary confinement.

I almost dropped my phone twice as I typed his number. I hung up once, then finally I let it ring. His deep tones travelled from my ear and sent spasms of sheer delight throughout my body.

I remember that voice. It still drips like honey in my memory.

~ ~ ~

A couple of weeks later, although it felt like mere hours and yet years all at once, we met for our first date. I took the day off work just to get prepared. I went to Sally's to get my hair done and bought a new dress from a little boutique on North Street, the alleyway leading to it was full of flowers, the florist next door was fulfilling a wedding order. It was through a sea of lilies, and the scent of lavender and a multitude of wild and vibrant plumes that I strode through the town. The steam from the vents came as clouds, I felt I was walking on air.

If only I had not been so lonely.

We met that night at Alfredo's on West Street at eight o'clock. The sun still hung in the sky painting the world in shades of gold and pink. We sat outside on the veranda overlooking a park filled with cherry blossoms, their petals covered the ground and swam in the air all around us. He wore dress pants and a short-sleeved shirt of the deepest blue, thick veiny forearms on display for the world to see. A black pencil tie accented with a golden floral design mirrored the flecks of gold in his deep brown eyes.

Those fleeting hours together spent drinking a little too much sparkling wine and eating some of the most wonderful pasta I have ever tasted, chatting away finally looking deep into each other's eyes as we did so will haunt me as a spectre of true happiness until my dying day. We were not two clumsy internet strangers who had mistaken relief of boredom for attraction, no he and I were more, this was more. Not a new love, but an ancient eldritch connection. There were no awkward silences, nothing that would tell you we had not been married for twenty years already.

And you tell me that waitress said I sat there alone that night? Impossible. Trust me, I know what it is like to be lonely, to be all alone in the world. This was not it, for the first time in what felt like an age, I was not alone. My heart knows he was there, my heart knows what we did that night. That night we made love in my apartment as the moon's light cascaded in from the open window, the gentle breeze played on my skin as he sent wave after wave of impulses throughout my being. I felt his strong body against my own frame, I heard his deep voice whisper softly in my ear as he nibbled at it speaking all the language of love I could ever want to hear. I thought I had known love, had known real passion with David, yet this night had taught me that it had been I, not his wife, who had been the lucky one. Where once just hearing his name would have caused a stir inside me now there was only indifference.

In the morning, he was gone. Only the scent of his aftershave—sandalwood and a light smoke, like hickory—remained on the sheets where he had lain. In the kitchen I found a wreath of dried foxtails forced into a heart shape with stained twine. To look upon it filled me with dread, but at the time I could not say why the blood in my veins turned to ice.

Then the rain began to fall.

~ ~ ~

All morning I called his number, but no answer ever came. No dialling tone, not a single word from the operator as to why, they said the number did not exist, that it was one digit too few. I went back to double check in our messages, but his account was gone. I went over and over our conversations, our actions, each word and every touch. There was no hint of anything wrong, had I done something wrong? Had I not been good enough the night before?

When have I ever been good enough?

The sky was black, and the rain hit the large umbrella hard as I walked to work. Figures surrounded me on all sides, jostling and jockeying for position, I let their pushes guide me along in their wake. A yellow cab sent a tidal wave of dirt and water through the air soaking my lower half to the bone. I did not care. As I reached the park below the balcony of Alfredo's, I stopped to gaze up at where we had sat. Cherry blossoms littered the floor, all dirt-stained pinks and browns as they began to rot away, the trees now skeletal, battered in the heavy winds. Then I saw it swaying in the wind hanging from the balcony rails, another—the same?—heart shaped wreath of purple foxtails. A flash of lightning caused me to jump and look to the floor, blinking away the searing lights etched into my vision. As the thunder rumbled I looked back, but the wreath was gone. I swear to you now that I saw a shadow from the corner of my eye moving between two buildings in the gloom, tall and well built—it was him I know it was.

I know it was him.

~ ~ ~

The hours without him slowly turned to days. I returned to my life—what there was of it—my usual routine, work to home and back. The skies would never clear. Life was bleak and the buildings drew in and closed out any hint of sunlight that tried to break through the high-walled concrete prison we found ourselves within. I longed for the summer days back in my little village, they felt so far away now. My longing led me back to those posts, the pictures where he had found me. The grief and loss weighed heavy upon my heart as I loaded up the final picture in the roll. This was the first one he had liked, although his name, his handsome face no longer in the list. My phone hit the floor in solidarity with my jaw; there, right there behind the smiling face of my mother, hanging from the well was a heart shaped wreath of foxtails.

Once I had regained my composure and retained my phone I zoomed in, unsure of what it all meant, had I been seeing things? Had I been hallucinating?

I know that is what you think, I can see it in your pitying eyes.

No, you have seen the picture, my mother confirmed it too, the foxtail wreath hung there illuminated in the sun's rays. Why do you deny the shadow I see in the picture is him? It is there as clear as the sky that day. That hint of gold, just to the left matches his tie. You say it is blurred, out of focus, a trick of the light, it could be anything—but I know, I know it was him.

You deem me crazy, but I know it to be true, it must be true. Who was he? How did he find me and why do I miss him still now? My heart feels empty once more, I am empty without him. Alone, yet again.

I did not know how to think or what to feel. How could I make sense of it all? If he had been there at the well dressing why had he not said a word about it? Thoughts rolled through my mind, one after the other: was I mistaken? Did he follow me? How did he find me? Why not approach me? No answers ever came, but the questions danced throughout my days.

Then I found the wreath on my desk.

Security could not answer the question of how it got there, no one could. I arrived at the office for a meeting with the editorial staff. I had been remote working for a while, anything to not step into that rain again, it had poured for as long as I could remember. It streamed down the windows as I stood over my desk, laying on top of the keyboard was the purple dried foxtail heart.

I tore from the building as fast as my legs would take me. Out on the street I scanned every face, every corner for a sight of him. My heart gave a leap and chilled all at once as I saw a shadow in the alleyway across the street. I did not know if I was terrified of finding him or driven by a need to see him again. Before my mind could decide how I felt about him, my feet had begun to cross the road.

It was between two dumpsters they found me; curled into a ball, the rain lashing down upon me, gathering all around me in the looming shadows as water cascaded from the harsh yellow plastic of the dumpsters I had wedged myself between. I was clutching a wreath of foxtail, but I did not see him.

You see, I had never told him where I worked.

~ ~ ~

As my forced leave from work—which had been enacted that very day—continued the rains finally stopped and the sun returned to our lives. This was not the sun of the summer, there was no warmth to it. This was not the same sun under which my mother and I arranged flowers, nor was it the sun that had made the sky dance brilliant colours as it set over a pasta date for two. This was a cruel imitation. Under its gaze was nothing but a chill in the cold light. It burnt away the clouds allowing the cold to seep into everything and everyone. The buildings of the city became ice covered behemoths, their shadows elongated and twisted, they mocked me. Every new dark corner was another place for him to hide, another place for him to follow me unseeing. I knew he was close, I always knew it—but he would never show himself.

Did I want him to?

I want him to even now.

I do not want him to, even now.

How I spent my days after the dumpster incident is a mystery to me. I was in half-life trapped between an anxiety and longing. All was consumed with thoughts of him. Some moments I would fear him as I nervously sat at the window staring down at the people passing by and peering into shadows. I would spend my time hugging the pillow where his scent lingered only in my deepest of memories. How long did I sit in my apartment scared he would find me, scared he would not be able to find me? I am told it was two weeks, until that morning.

If only I had stayed inside.

I remember waking that day and feeling like my head was clear for the first time in what felt like an age. A traveller stepping out of a fog to find themselves already at their destination. I cleaned, I showered, I ate—or at least tried to, but food was not plentiful, how had I been existing? Had I been existing at all? That is what took me out of the apartment that day, not thoughts of him, not a longing nor a fear—a trip to the coffee shop. The streets were emptier than my refrigerator, a snowfall was keeping everyone who was not already at work firmly inside. I waded through the dirtied slush armed with a cappuccino and onion bagel. I walked the streets without purpose allowing the fresh cold air to fill my lungs and turn my cheeks that refreshing kind of numb. I felt almost myself again. I reached the park next to Alfredo's, not that I had planned to go near the place and instead of fear or dread I simply stood and watched the snow gathering on the skeletal branches of the cherry blossoms, it was beauty and peace.

I should not have stopped.

There is no beauty, there is no peace without him.

A glint of gold moving behind a thickened oak tree caught my eye, I squinted to look closer and the Styrofoam cup fell from my hand turning the pristine snow muddy and brown. I ran toward the tree unthinking, I had one goal in mind, one mission.

Him.

I tore it from the tree in a thrill of ecstasy that was matched only by the dread forming in the pit of my stomach, for there pinned to the oak was his tie, the golden floral pattern on deepest black gripped tight in my hand. It smelled of sandalwood and hickory, of him, of our night together. A chill that had nothing to do with the snow travelled up my spine as I saw shadows moving amongst the trees. I followed them through the park and out through the rusted gate that led to the other side of town. The buildings here were smaller and packed together, they boxed me in like a great labyrinth, but I was never lost; at each turn, at every corner a hint of him. I knew I was getting closer; his scent filled my nostrils as I sped up to meet him. A light was dead ahead where the buildings parted, and as I broke through their darkness I was covered in sweat; it was time, finally time to see him again, to know the truth.

He was not there.

I gave a great cry into the empty street. He had evaded me again—that is when I saw it on the bridge overlooking the railway and I finally knew where my answers lay. As I climbed to meet it, I heard voices of people around me, they seemed to be gathering, shouting, but I did not care nor listen. One tried to grab at me, and I slapped her so hard she fell to the floor, yet the pain in my hand did not faze me, it barely registered. At the top of the bridge I stood on my tiptoes to detach the foxtail wreath and once free, I clutched it tight to my breast as tears streamed from my eyes. In that moment I knew the answer—there was not a single doubt in my mind.

I jumped.

When I awoke it was not to answers, it was not to him, it was to doubt and to pain. The constant fear and poking and prodding of you and your doctors, and—well, you know the rest. How dare you, how dare anyone try to convince me that this was not real and that I am mad!

I am not mad.

Am I mad?

I do not think I am mad.

~ ~ ~

"That is her version of the events at any rate," Dr. McKeath clicked the stop button on the tape recorder and turned to the pale-faced couple holding hands across from her. "I fear your daughter had a severe mental break, it is not uncommon for young people in the city who find themselves alone to live a fantasy life of sorts, but in loneliness she's created a delusion which—"

"So, we're sure this fella isn't real then?"

"Arthur, we've gone over this again and again, of course he isn't real. The police never found anyone, the waitress saw her alone, the receipt in her apartment for the tie—Oh, my poor baby girl, I have let her down."

"Now please. You must not blame yourselves, and rest easy she is in safe hands now."

"When can we take her home?"

"It shouldn't be much longer now. We just need to wait for her legs to heal and the casts to come off and then we can start thinking about day release."

"I just want her home with us, away from the city and from this."

"Mrs. Liverly, the problem is in Stacey's mind. Her physical injuries from the jump are severe, but they are a symptom not the cause."

"She's right, Jill. She's yours, Doc, for as long as she needs to be." Arthur Liverly reached out to take his wife's hand in his own. "Let's go see her," he added what he hoped was a reassuring pressure to his grip. "Don't forget to smile for her."

The group made their way through the medical facility. Row upon row of blue doors down pristine white corridors led them to the critical care unit and to Stacey Liverly's door. The doctor knocked to give her warning of their entrance, but there was no reply. Undeterred, Dr. McKeath swiped her key card and they entered.

"What's going on? Where is she?"

"I—I don't know," Dr. McKeath's heels clicked loudly as she ran back out into the corridor. "Nurse, nurse!"

Arthur placed his hands firmly on Jill's shoulders, "It's okay, love. They'll find her, they will. She can't have gotten far. Not in those casts."

Jill could not speak; her mouth fell open and her eyes widened as she raised her hand to point at the bed. Propped against the pillow was a heart shaped wreath of foxtails.

BOOM

by

IOANNA ARKA

How long have we been waiting? Emily is asleep on my arms, and my back hurts as I sit here on a rickety three-legged stool, supporting thirty pounds of snot and rosy cheeks and soft snores. It would have been a precious moment, if not for the absurdity of what transpired a few hours ago.

The men with the suits and the earpieces have opened both doors and the single narrow window, but the ovens were busy the whole morning, and there's little chance the room will get cooler before night comes. We've taken all the muffins out, but they wouldn't let us resume our business. There won't be enough cupcakes for Monday's customers. If they still come, that is. If the Secret Service allows us to open that soon after . . .

I shake my head to clear it of the intrusive memories of that horrible scene. I think of the one thing that always calms me down: Max.

~ ~ ~

Our math teacher's histrionic outbreaks were a thing to behold. Ms. Gagarin would throw her book on her desk and ask herself—or us, or maybe the universe, it was never really clear who the anger was directed at—why she even bothered with the likes of us. We didn't understand anything, no matter how hard she worked, and we were unlikely to ever learn. She was busting her ass trying to pull us through, in the hopes that some few of us would make it to college, but did we listen? Did we care? Nobody ever dared—or bothered—answering the rhetorical question, and so she kept shouting, and we kept looking awkwardly at the floor, the desks, each other, until the bell rang and we could escape the raging harpy.

I had learned to expect the thump of the book that introduced these outbreaks by Max's gentle tap on my shoulder. Ms. Gagarin, when in one of her sour moods, was prone to stroll around the classroom, looking for students' notebooks to grab and peruse. Their contents were proof that we were a bunch of imbeciles, unlikely to ever achieve proficiency in the universal language of mathematics. Max's tap was the signal to summarily dispose of any non-mathematical notes on my desk, especially the little cheesy love notes I liked passing him during the boring math periods, and feign undivided attention to Ms. Gagarin's lecture.

I'm not sure how he always read her moods so well. It was just one of those things you accept when you're young, in those malleable years before you learn to be a skeptic. After all, there was no reason to doubt his nearly psychic abilities: he was always right, and that was proof enough for me. The quiet, thoughtful boy I loved could read minds, or that's what we said when we joked about it.

Max and I got married directly after high school, and by the time he finished college, we were ready to have a family. It was all furniture-store-catalog perfect: the pregnancy, the birth of our beautiful daughter, the little house we rented, our fresh and content home life. Somehow, I had known it would be exactly like that, because Max hadn't been worried at all through this. He was the emotional barometer of our little universe. As long as he was calm, everything was going to be all right.

That changed one Sunday, eight months after Emily's birth.

The baby had been fussy all morning, and to make it all worse, Max wouldn't stop complaining about the worst headache of his life. He never had headaches, and if I'm absolutely honest, I really didn't need his grumbling while I dealt with a child that needed to be held twenty-four-seven. Sleep deprived for months, my nipples raw from breastfeeding—the little devil wouldn't take the bottle—I resented his unwillingness to look after her for a little longer than the time it took me to use the bathroom. And I resented the baby, too: why couldn't she stop screaming bloody murder when she was in her dad's arms? Still, *her* I couldn't reason with. As for him, a little before noon my patience finally gave out, and I told him to get out of my way until his headache was gone. If he couldn't help me, then at least he should leave me alone.

And leave me alone he did. When Emily fell asleep that afternoon, I lay down on the bed we'd shared for the past six years only to discover that my husband wasn't breathing. He was still warm to the touch, and I called an ambulance, but there was nothing they could do, and he was declared dead on arrival. Probably an aneurysm, a doctor said as my conscience floated over a numb version of myself sitting in a dismal hospital corridor later that evening. Her face showed all the outward signs of compassion, but the floating version of me detected a certain detachment about her—she'd done this before, and she'd do it again, and although she felt for me, she wouldn't let herself get affected by yet another tragedy.

And what about that person slumped in the inadequate plastic waiting room chair, the woman in jogging pants and a stained t-shirt, who had a sleeping baby sprawled across her? The consciousness floating over the three females—all in different stages of their lives, all with different cares in their minds—marveled at the stillness of the moment, the child sunken in that peaceful, untroubled sleep of babies, the dazed mother with the pale, blank face, and the doctor who waited, patience and a vague expression of resignation etched on her face. *This will be the last calm moment for a while,* the floating version of myself thought. Very soon it would have to plunge back into the pale woman, and then the horror would hit us both, and all the things that needed to be taken care of would crash on us like an angry mob.

The baby stirred and rubbed her face on the sprawled figure's chest, and the two parts of me merged in a collision that was no less jarring for the fact that I'd been expecting it. I moved Emily up so that she could rest her head on my shoulder and sat up on the chair. After a deep inhalation and a long, bracing exhalation, I looked up at the doctor's face.

"What do I do now?"

In a calm voice, she explained to me the steps that should be taken. I listened and paid attention, and then with a commiserating pursing of the lips, she was gone.

I tried not to dwell on how horrible I'd been to him in the last hours of his life—how could I have possibly known?—but the floodgates finally collapsed when I discovered the insurance policy among his papers. I cried and cried, now holding Emily and pacing around the living room, huddled with her in the bed that was much too large for me. I don't know why a healthy twenty-four-year-old man had seen fit to buy life insurance. Was it his sixth sense? Had he felt his death coming, the same way he'd felt others' moods? Had it been the same talent that warned him something was about to go wrong, or was it just his organized, diligent nature that had made him tick all the boxes before having a family?

~ ~ ~

The Secret Service man who's standing next to my oven lets out a little cough, and my attention snaps back to the here and now.

The equipment that surrounds me, the shop, the success, it was all Max's doing. The insurance policy provided the capital, my emotional struggles after his death the concept. And so, out of adversity and death-transcending love, Mandy's Mood Cupcakes was born. Vanilla for those busy ones heading for another normal day at work, lemon for the happy, cheery folks, lavender for those who felt blue—the mild, flowery fragrance is guaranteed to smooth down the sadness into a sweet melancholy. Swedish-style cardamom and cinnamon for lovebirds. The customers are happy. The bakery, a tribute to Max's ability to read the feelings of those around him, has been a huge success.

Until today.

~ ~ ~

This morning, I woke up earlier than usual, like I always do when a busy, stressful day awaits me. A faint mirage of Max still lingered in the drowsy recesses of my mind as I got up to make my usual morning coffee. He's been visiting me often in my dreams. When he comes to me, I tell him about Emily, our little struggles as she grows and learns, her quirks, and all the ways she reminds me of him. Sometimes, he gives me advice, an idea about a new cupcake flavor, a soothing word that smooths the turbulent waves of my emotions, when life with a business and a demanding toddler becomes too exhausting. Upon awakening, I'm always left with a feeling of sweet nostalgia, and the days that start with Max's memory are always lavender with a tinge of lemon.

This time, though, the image of him was slipping too fast, and the feeling wouldn't leave me that there was something important, a crucial bit of information, something I had to keep, a message that needed to be preserved. Rubbing my eyes, still groggy and half-asleep and not really knowing what I was doing, I fished out a notepad from a kitchen drawer and scrawled down the words before they slipped away. The sense of urgency receded, and I started preparing my coffee.

As the hot water made its rounds in my drip coffee machine, I turned on the TV, hoping to catch in the morning shows a mention of our little town. We aren't really known for anything, but by a stroke of luck Cranfield, Arizona found itself on the President's campaign trail, and one of his aides, who's from the area, mentioned my little cupcake shop.

My shop. The President would visit *my* little bakery. Maybe I should start a franchise after that. Business has been going so well, after all. Maybe this will be the first day of the rest of my life.

"The White House press secretary reassured the nation this morning that the latest missile test isn't considered an act of aggression, and the President hasn't canceled any events on the campaign trail. But let's welcome our military analyst, Sean Johnson. Sean, what do you think? Are we on the verge of a nuclear . . ."

"Boom!"

I had nearly tuned out the sound of the TV, lost in daydreams of culinary success, but Emily's voice brought me back to the present. She stood in the doorway of the living room, pointing at the screen, where the anchor and the analyst kept discussing the range of the missiles North Korea had been testing for the past couple of days.

"Boom!" she said again in her tiny, squeaky voice. Her hand pointed at the screen. "Boom!"

I should be more careful, I thought to myself. Who knew what could scare a small child? She didn't really have to watch stock videos of missile launches playing in the background of a newsreel. I switched off the TV, walked over to her, and crouched down so that my eyes were level with hers.

"Good morning, darling! Big day today. We're going to mama's bakery."

"Boom!"

"Don't worry, sweetie, that was nothing."

"Daddy said boom."

My breathing stopped for a second or two, but I got my bearings soon enough. I scooped the child up in my arms, leaving a kiss on her warm cheek. *Kids*, I thought, willing the sudden pang of unease away. *You never know what'll come out of their mouths.* It wasn't strange, was it? She knew that most of her friends had daddies. She'd seen a man on TV. Maybe she thought all men were called "Daddy." What did she know? She was only three.

"What do you want for breakfast? Cereal?"

"No, toast."

"All right, sweetie, let's make some toast. Mommy will have a cup of coffee, and then we have to go to work. I'll dress you up today, the President is coming."

My knees creaked as I walked to the kitchen with her in my arms. I put her down on the kitchen counter and looked for my favorite mug in the cupboard over her head. As I set it down, my eyes landed on the small post-it. I picked it up and perused the words I had already half forgotten: *Emily knows.*

I shook my head. *Wonderful. Messages in dreams. Next, I'll believe in fairies.* I ripped off the paper and threw it in the bin.

~ ~ ~

The agent's walkie-talkie springs to life. He turns his face to the side and exchanges some words with the person on the other end of the transmission. I can't understand much behind all the crackling—not that I'm paying attention. I've been drifting through memories of my dead husband and of the lucid dreams that soothe me even as I know I'll wake up and have to face life without him again.

Another one of those, long forgotten, springs up in my thoughts. We're sitting on a lakeshore—not a place I recognize—and an older version of Emily jumps around in the shallows. She must be five or six years old, but it doesn't feel strange. Her hair is a tone darker than the very light blonde her curls now have; and straighter, too.

"I'll always look after you," he says. *"I'll chase the dangers away. You'll be safe."*

Strange. I have no memory of waking up from that dream. No idea when it was. It's not one of the recurring ones—in those, Emily is always as I know her. In that irrational way these things go, it helps to know that Max can see her grow up through his manifestations in my sleeping mind. Although, that's, of course, absurd. Max is dead. He can't see Emily. He can't see anything.

My eyes drift to my pastry chef. Jen is sitting on another hard stool across the big work table on which rows of muffins are cooling—have probably cooled by now—absentmindedly nursing a sore thumb. She was hard at work when we came in this morning, late, because Emily is in that phase where no outfit is good enough for her, and not finding her favorite socks can induce a thirty-minute-long tantrum. I wouldn't have brought her to work, not today of all days, but it's one of those things that just happens: babysitter sick, no substitute to be found on such short notice.

The Secret Service was here when I arrived, but they've already vetted us and checked the place beforehand. I set Emily up with pencils and coloring books and went to work. Busy day. The President was coming. The publicity we'd get from this was priceless. God, how my heart was beating. Everything had to be perfect.

Still, I took a second to close my eyes and breathe in deeply. Max's face drifted to the inside of my eyelids. He'd be so proud.

The man's device disappears somewhere in his suit. His body returns to its familiar, rigid pose, and his eyes scan the room in a quick, perfunctory arc before settling on me.

"It won't be long now, miss. We'll know soon." He nods, perhaps in an attempt to ease my mind. He must understand that this whole day has tested my sanity to the extreme. I look at the large clock. It's long past Emily's bedtime. The sun has set, but that was already clear from the quickly fading light outside the back door.

My thoughts shift back to the events of that morning.

~ ~ ~

"Boo boo!" Emily said.

Shit, what now? Another scrape? I don't have time for this. The President would be here soon. How much longer? What time had they said?

I bit down a sting of guilt at my less-than-motherly thought and walked over to her. She'd been good all morning, drawing and watching videos on my phone. Busy as I was, Emily came first. Emily would always come first, even if it was just a boo boo.

"Are you all right, honey? Did you hurt yourself?"

She was still sitting at the low side table. I examined her face, her hands. No blood. No crying. Had I heard correctly?

"Boo boo," she said again. She stretched her short arm, a pudgy little finger pointing across the room to where Jen was taking a large tray of fresh muffins out of one of the ovens.

"Shit!" The hot tray landed on the table with a loud *clank*. I watched, unable to react as it skidded along the metal surface and came to a stop at the edge, barely missing the tipping point. Jen had ripped off her oven mitts and was holding her hand under the running tap, emitting obscenities at the mischievous deities of kitchen injuries.

A Special Forces man peeked in the doorway. "Everything all right?"

I stared at him, unsure if things were, indeed, all right.

"It's fine, it's fine, I just burned my hand," Jen answered. "Everything's fine. We're almost ready."

I looked at Emily, who didn't seem at all disturbed by the rattle, the shouts, or the fact that Jen had been injured and was obviously in pain. I looked at the tray, perching precariously on the edge of the table, some muffins toppled over. I looked at the discarded oven mitt, lying on the floor. I picked it up. There was a hole in the thumb. Had Emily seen it? How could she have possibly known?

You know how, a voice whispered inside my mind. A tap on the shoulder, a warning before things went south. Strange, I could have sworn that my thoughts sounded a lot like Max, lately.

At least the muffins were safe. Thinking of it now, that was the least of my problems.

All was in place when the motorcade arrived, early that afternoon. I allowed myself a last quick inspection of the place. There were fresh flowers in the vases on the little round tables, and the motley rows of cupcakes—mostly the "happy" ones, today—neatly arranged behind the spotless glass of the counter display, awaited new admirers. An assortment sat on the tray on the counter by the till; another agent in a dark suit stood guard over them, never leaving them out of sight. They were the ones the President himself could taste. The Secret Service had watched us prepare them that morning, asking us questions about the ingredients—some of them idiotic, if you asked me, but who knows what they have to check for. I'd made a point of licking batter and buttercream off my fingers and jested that I'd take a bite out of every cupcake on the tray, if that would ease their paranoia.

The bakery got overfull and stiflingly hot even before the President entered. Lights, cameras, noise. I picked up Emily and held her in my arms, afraid she'd get overstimulated and have a meltdown at this inopportune time. But she was fine. More than fine, really: she watched on with interest, eyes glued to the Secret Service men and the smiling President, ambling towards us in the midst of reporters and smiles from my small staff.

"Boom!" said Emily. Her left arm was stretched towards the approaching group of people, but she wasn't pointing with her finger. She couldn't point because something was clamped in her clenched fist.

"What's that, honey? What do you have there?"

"A present," she replied. "For the man go boom!"

I tried to shift her to my left arm so that I could look in her hand, but she was heavy, and the President had already reached the counter with the closely guarded cupcakes. Somebody whispered something in his ears, pointing in my direction. The leader of the free world looked at me and smiled.

"Oh, are these all for me?"

"Yes sir!" I said, a little too enthusiastically. "You can take them home, if you like."

"Oh, wow." He took a step in my direction. "And who's this little one?"

"This is Emily."

"Hi, Emily," he said in that drawn out, over-cheery voice people use when they talk to small children. "Do you like mommy's cupcakes?"

"They're okay."

Everybody laughed.

"OK, you wanna share one?" he asked her. "Which is your favorite flavor?"

"I have jelly beans!" She opened her outstretched hand, and lo and behold, there rested five little blobs of candy, a little too glossy, I thought, probably because it was hot and she was sweating. I winced. *Where did she get those? At least I made her wash her hands beforehand.* She wasn't too grubby today, thank heavens.

The President took it all in stride.

"Really? Which are your favorites?"

"All of them!"

"Oh, wow, can't argue with that. Can I have one?"

"Yes, but only one!"

He let out a short laugh and picked one.

"Thank you, honey. And, you know what, maybe someday you'll visit the White House, and you can try our candy!" He popped the jelly bean in his mouth and smiled at her.

"Yay!" she shouted, clenching her fists and throwing her head back and her hands up, one of them barely missing my nose. I nearly fell forward, and I struggled to maintain my balance—a heavy toddler doing acrobatics in your arms is not easy business—and this brought me face to face with the President.

That's weird, I thought to myself. His eyes had gone wide and were fixed on mine. No sound came out of his mouth. Indeed, I wasn't sure he was breathing.

I took a step back. Right there, before my eyes, he stretched a hand towards the agent closest to him, grabbing the muscular man's shoulder, while the other one migrated to his throat. The expression of surprise on his face disturbed me, although I couldn't exactly say why.

I don't remember much after that. Someone elbowed me, hard, and I stumbled back, grateful to bump against a wall before I fell on my behind. Emily was still in my arms, silently watching the chaos that had erupted before our eyes; phones, walkie-talkies, shouts, people shoved to the side, Secret Service herding everyone out, and already—how was it even possible?—the sound of sirens in the distance.

I slid down the wall and sat there, on the floor, an eerily calm child still in my arms, my eyes glued to two well-polished shoes attached to a supine male form. Three people stooped over him, and by the periodic jerking of one of those bent bodies, I knew they were trying to resuscitate him.

The paramedics barged in soon after that.

"Choked on a jelly bean, Heimlich didn't help, CPR for three minutes," the bent agent with the periodically jerking shoulders barked as they lifted the unmoving body onto a stretcher and disappeared out the front door of my bakery. They'd cracked it, I realized. The glass in my front door was cracked.

I took a breath and tried to get up, but my legs weren't cooperating. Emily shimmied out of my arms and picked up one of her jelly beans that had fallen on the floor. *Don't eat that!* I wanted to shout, but my voice, much like the rest of me, was just not ready.

~ ~ ~

His phone rings, and he listens to the person on the other end of the line before he puts it back in his inner jacket pocket. When he turns to me, his face has the same stony expression he has been wearing the whole time.

"You can go home, miss."

Oh, thank God. Those were the longest six hours of my life.

~ ~ ~

The coffee machine is gurgling, my coffee will be ready soon. Emily is still sleeping, exhausted, the poor thing, from all the excitements of yesterday. As I turn on the TV, I glimpse through my living room window the black car on the other side of the street. But they won't stay long. He choked, they said. They just have to stay here until the toxicology report comes out, clearing me of any foul play.

I sit down on my sofa and turn up the volume. I still hope to get a glimpse of my bakery in the footage from yesterday's tragic events. Am I a bad person? I don't think I am. And there's not much mention of Cranfield, anyway. North Korea has launched another test missile.

"A source in the White House told us that President Collins sketched out a counterattack plan, including a possible nuclear counterstrike. Now, is it true that President McLean already ruled out the possibility of a swift counter-attack?"

"Yes, Mark. Let's remind the viewers who just tuned in that President McLean, vice-president until yesterday, was sworn in yesterday evening, soon after President Collins was declared dead after choking on a piece of candy while on the campaign

trail in Cranfield, Arizona. But now, over to our correspondent in Washington, DC, for more details on the ongoing crisis and the new President's plans."

"Thank you, David. Apparently, President Collins put the US Strategic Command on high alert two days ago, on Saturday. Multiple strikes on military targets in North Korea were planned as a response to a possible provocation in the next few days. Now, we don't know if the possibility of nuclear . . ."

"Mommy?"

I switch off the TV and turn to look at Emily, standing in the doorway, her stuffed whale in her hand. I smile at her. My little angel, so innocent; she has no idea what her jelly beans caused.

"Good morning, honey."

"No more boom," she says. "The bad man. He ate my jelly bean. Now he can't go boom."

Something in her tone makes me slightly queasy. I swallow down the unwelcome sensation, the sudden, unexpected suspicion. It can't be true.

"Sweetie, where did you find those jelly beans?"

"Daddy gave them to me."

"What did daddy look like?"

"He looked like daddy. Like always."

I pause, feeling my heartbeat accelerating. *Concentrate on your breathing*, I tell myself. *Slowly. In, out. Emily shouldn't see you hyperventilate.*

"Do you know daddy's name?" I ask her as calmly as I can.

"He said daddy was Max. Now it's only daddy."

I press my lips together, trying to blink back tears. "Did daddy say anything else to you, honey?"

"He said, I love you."

I squint, straining to keep everything inside, but there's no holding back the flood anymore. Emily walks over to me, thrusts the whale in my direction. I barely see the stuffed thing behind the blurry saltiness in my eyes.

"Don't be sad, mommy. Whale is here."

I take her in my arms and squeeze her against my breast, as tight as I can without hurting her, burying my face in her curls, breathing in her soft and powdery baby-head smell. And right then, my eyes wander to the window, and through the fuzziness of my tears and the stroboscopic effect of the sunlight seeping through the shifting foliage outside, I swear a male silhouette flickers just beyond the grasp of my earthly senses, and a voice whispers in the back of my mind:

"You'll always be safe."

ALTERNATIVE MEDICINE

by

NATALIE PINTER

"**Y**ou can take the blindfold off now," Dominic said, turning the car off.

Naomi untied the kerchief, rubbed her eyes, and looked around. It was almost pitch dark, and from the sensation of riding on long, winding gravel roads, she knew they were in the middle of nowhere.

Anais told me it would be weird. She wouldn't have sent me to them if it wasn't worth it.

And I have to do it. I have to do it for Samantha.

Dominic had picked her up at the appointed time the day after she'd called the number on the card. "Tomorrow. Midnight." He'd had an accent—maybe Hungarian. She'd been watching for the red Sedan from the window for forty minutes. When he'd finally pulled up, she'd kissed a sleeping Samantha, and left. Dominic had parked and stood on the sidewalk, waiting for her. He was shorter than she was, and gaunt. He looked to be in his fifties, and beneath his fine suit was a wiry frame. His eyes were pale, clear blue.

"You have the money? Yes, good." He'd smiled, and Naomi felt a lurch in her stomach at the scarcity of teeth in his mouth.

Meth addict? Carny? Seriously, Anais?

On the road he'd said, "Do what I say and don't ask questions. Give me your cell phone."

She'd hesitated. "I'd really rather not."

"I return when we are done. We don't take chances. You could take picture." He smelled like cigarettes, and something else, almost like a barn.

Halfway through the ride, when they were on the freeway, he'd tossed the blindfold in the backseat, and when she balked at putting it on he'd threatened to pull over and drop her off on the side of the road. She reminded herself that Anais had said she'd been scared too. And so Naomi acquiesced. She wasn't sure how long they'd been riding for, but it felt like at least an hour. "Where are we going?"

"Don't ask questions."

Then he'd taken out his phone and spoke to someone in a language she couldn't place. It sounded somewhere between Portuguese and Italian, which was odd as she'd thought his accent was Eastern European.

Naomi stepped out of the car. Trees surrounded a path they walked down, and in the distance, she could make out a couple of trailers. She tilted her head low so that she could breathe heavily into her scarf to warm herself. She wished for the hundredth time that they were doing this in the daytime. And why had she worn heels, for fuck's sake? Eighties heavy metal seeped out from speakers from the first trailer they passed, along with the scent of cigarettes and pot, and the jabber of low, sanguine voices. Beams of light in the roof cut through the darkness and gleamed off Dominic's bald spot.

Naomi was walking so fast that she was generating some heat despite the chill. She clutched a couple of loose pills in her pocket, wishing she could pop one, but with her gloves on she was afraid of dropping it, and they were walking too fast. Her doctor had only prescribed her a few precious Xanax, and it wasn't worth the risk of losing one. She would have to force herself to breathe slowly and power through what felt like a looming panic attack.

They won't hurt me. They didn't hurt Anais, and they want my money—the rest of my money—too much.

She'd already paid so much it made her feel sick to think it wouldn't work. Dominic didn't even glance over his shoulder to see that she was still there. He just expected her to keep up. Of course she would. Naomi would do anything.

~ ~ ~

Anais said the methods might be different. Very *Alternative medicine*, she'd called it. Naomi didn't know where her friend had found these people. "I believe there are different kinds of . . . options. But whatever it is, you have to . . . *do* it yourself. And don't ask them questions. They hate that."

"Okay, what would I be *doing* though? Like sacrificing a goat?" Naomi had laughed, nervous and baffled that Anais was being so cagey.

Dominic had collected a large sum from Naomi last week. And he would get more "after."

~ ~ ~

Naomi grasped absent-mindedly for the phone that wasn't still in her pocket. She took deep breaths, trying to ignore the tug of maternal tethers, growing taut being far from Samantha, and in a strange place. She wished she was back at home. Or even in the hospital—familiar and dreary—near her daughter. She would return as soon as she could, though surely Sam was still sleeping. *But what if she wakes up and needs me? Or what if I need her?* Samantha's presence was equally comforting to her. They were a team—symbiotic in so many ways. The sympathetic stress had even caused her to lose weight and hair just like her little girl.

Dominic reached the last trailer. This one darker—more of the lights were out and she realized they were moving towards the edge and the trees beyond.

A teenage boy was lurking around the side of the trailer and walked up to Dominic. "She's still awake," he said angrily in the same accent as Dominic.

~ ~ ~

She had the feeling there was something that would have an even greater cost than the money she'd already shelled out. But Anais had said they would help. They would help Sam as they'd helped her son, Lukas. Lukas was better—a miraculous recovery the doctors had proclaimed it—although Anais didn't seem much happier for some reason. She'd looked haunted when she'd pulled the card from her pocket and hesitantly given it to Naomi. They'd met at the bar across the street from the hospital where the two tired mothers had sipped bourbon and stared out at the rain pounding against the glass, both giving off the vibe of being utterly unapproachable.

The rain outside had made the street and buildings warbly. Since Sam's diagnosis, two years ago, the world had changed. Its colors and patterns. The sense of reality. Things felt blurry, mutable. Sickening fear and potential heartbreak looming so close made reality elastic. Everything was more present and precious. Naomi was not religious, but she now understood why people were. Her daughter's existence was intensified against the backdrop of their circumstances. Sam was a sweet child, more dreamy than precocious. And she understood what was happening to her, and was frightened. Her daughter was a shining miraculous thing from the moment she'd appeared in Naomi's arms, slippery and newborn. She had been such a good baby. Even a good toddler. And Naomi might lose her in a few months or a few years. Naomi lied awake at night and made desperate bargains with a deity she only vaguely believed in.

~ ~ ~

She felt cold just looking at the teenage boy standing there in his thin t-shirt. Dominic barked something at him again. The boy grunted at him in reply and to Naomi he said insolently, "Why would you be part of it?"

Dominic spoke again, angrily pointing toward the trailer. Then in English, he spat, "Go get Fortuna and make coffee."

Naomi dug one of her high heels into the dirt and glanced around furtively. She had a chance now to quickly remove her glove, fish out a pill, and pop one under her tongue.

The door creaked open and an older woman with a bun of black hair, streaked with iron-gray, assessed her. She cocked her head to the right and spoke to Dominic in that mystery language, sprinkling the word 'Damien' throughout.

Naomi shivered.

Dominic pulled out a pack of cigarettes, put one in his mouth and held the pack out to the old woman who reached for one. "Yes, he already told you," he said, lighting her cigarette before his.

Fortuna, took a long drag and addressed Naomi, "You got a sick kid?"

Naomi nodded. "My daughter, she's nine. Leukemia." Her voice used to quaver when she told people this, but it was a year on and she'd gotten used to the word and so, so tired of the crumpled brows, the gasps, and hands-to-the-heart. The offers of sympathy and the pitying gazes. Worst of all, the looks of fear. That veiled feeling of being a pariah. As if Naomi had some pathology of misfortune they could catch. It all bespoke of the hopelessness she fought so hard against.

Fortuna stepped down from the porch and they all followed her to the side of the trailer to the little fenced-in area where the teenage boy had appeared from. At the end of the yard was a small barn and several feet to the right of it stood another smaller structure. Between these was a slender wooden table with a small handsaw. The smaller building looked like a large kennel. A misty light, strangely soothing, shimmered through the slats.

The woman went up to the structure and Naomi could see something through the bars of the cage but it wasn't clear. Fortuna spoke in a low voice to whatever was in the cage, made a clucking sound with her tongue, and then turned and looked at Naomi with twinkling eyes. She waved her over. Hesitantly, Naomi walked towards the kennel and looked through the bars at the source of the aura.

The world expanded and contracted. Naomi felt like she'd just stepped off a merry-go-round. The creature inside was the size of a Great Dane and shaped like a delicate horse. It looked at her and she could have fallen into those large, heavily lashed, obsidian eyes like a well.

It made a shivery "neigh" but she could imagine it speaking the language of all living things of this world and others. The shimmering spiral between the creature's eyes was *in motion*—a slow, perpetual twirl like the ballerina that popped up and pirouetted when Sam opened her little jewelry box.

"Horn is panacea," said Fortuna, blowing out a trail of smoke.

"What?" Naomi was panting and her breath was fogging the air. Her peripheral vision sparkled. She still felt the pill, hard and bitter—not dissolving fast enough—beneath her tongue. She didn't know what she'd been expecting; black magic? Not this.

Naomi took a step closer. "I don't understand." She forced herself to look at Fortuna. Then she blinked and turned to the table next to the cage with the little handsaw and shuddered.

"It drinks nectar. We added potion. Should sleep soon."

The creature made a noise, a desperate whimper, looking back and forth between the two women. Fortuna addressed it in that strange language. The creature shook its head back and forth, collapsed onto delicate forelegs, and looked up at Naomi with those angelic, liquid eyes.

It knows, Naomi thought. *It knows what we're saying.*

"What . . . will happen to it?"

The woman turned to her. "Strong beast. Immortal essence in the horn."

My god, Sam. Her daughter loved all animals. And she *adored* unicorns. They were painted on the border of her bedroom walls. She had t-shirts and figurines. She loved them more than mermaids and ponies.

"I'm sorry, what?" Naomi laughed. Somehow she had started the evening in one world and ended up in another place she didn't recognize. She'd been prepared for something strange, perhaps unethical, but not something that upended reality. Was this even real? Was it a solution? She stepped forward and ran her fingertips along the saw. "Why can't someone else do it?"

The woman said something to Dominic. She sounded irritated. And addressed Naomi. "You paid for something that work."

"Where did you get this creature?"

"No questions," Dominic reminded her sharply.

"You only need little," Fortuna said, holding up her thumb and forefinger and bringing them almost together but leaving a little space.

"But a little bit will kill it, yes?" Naomi bit her lip. This was her chance to save Sam and she might be squandering it with her hesitancy and her questions. "I don't

. . . give me a moment." Naomi's knees were weak. Her hands trembled. When she looked at the saw again, she stumbled a few feet back.

The boy had walked around the back from the entrance and said something sharply to Dominic and Fortuna. He pointed at the cage and his voice warbled.

Dominic yelled something and then gestured to Fortuna and they both stepped back into the trailer, muttering. He leaned out the door and in English said to the boy: "You stay out of this. I told you."

The boy turned to her frowning and mumbled something.

"What?" she whispered.

"It's a sin." he said through clenched teeth.

"It's not possible," she whispered. "You people are a whole other level of shady. Who the hell has access to such a thing and what kind of person does this?"

The boy snorted. "*You* don't know what is possible." He glanced down at the trailer. "I'm too late. You should look into her eyes. Doing the job when she falls asleep . . ." He shook his head. "That is the coward's way. Don't do it unless you are willing to look into her eyes." He sat down on an overturned paint bucket and clutched his head in his hands. "I was so close."

"So close to what?" whispered Naomi.

"To saving her." He looked at her again. "They are using you to do the dirty work. Worried about their souls." He rolled his eyes. "As if bringing you here and making you do it doesn't count."

"But I . . . I don't think I can."

He lifted his head and blinked up at her. She couldn't read his expression well in the dark. "They would be sure you would . . . but"—he continued, quickly standing back up—"if you just bring your daughter here maybe . . . Dominic wants someone to take the horn because they can turn it to powder. They would make so much money."

How many times had she and Anais discussed their desperation? Said to one another that they'd do anything, give anything, to make their children well—to save them. "Will . . . will it work?" she asked the boy. He did look young. How many times had she looked at her daughter and worried if she would grow up?

He glanced around again. They heard Dominic muttering something inside. "Give me your number," he said suddenly. "Leave. Tell them you won't. They won't be able to find another person too soon. It will give me time."

She patted herself down again and said, "Dominic took my phone. We'll have to use yours."

He shook his head. "I don't have one. I'll have to use Tony's when he gets back."

Naomi glanced around. She heard Fortuna say something and laugh inside the trailer. A witch's cackle. "Do you have a pen and paper?"

The boy shook his head. "Tell it to me quick, I'll remember."

Who was Tony and what kind of kid that age didn't have their own phone?

The door opened and she whispered the phone number quickly under her breath.

The boy nodded, closed his eyes, and whispered it back to her.

"Yes."

He continued mouthing the numbers, nodding to himself, frowning in concentration.

The trailer's back door flapped open and Dominic came back outside, followed by Fortuna. He said to the boy in English, "You stay out of this. I told you. Make more coffee."

The boy looked at her pointedly for a beat, and then disappeared through the door.

Naomi took a deep breath and stepped closer and gazed into the kennel. She was reminded of how she felt one morning after college when she'd gone backpacking through Europe and was standing before the Reims cathedral in France at sunrise. That awareness of being in the presence of something magnificent and sacred. How she felt seeing Sam on the ultrasound for the first time. Moments that she cherished as sublime. Holy.

She shifted her gaze to the handsaw and then back to the creature, now sagging against the wall. Its eyes were drooping but open and full of mysteries and wild wonders—like the void of the night sky. The windows into a vast, immortal soul. And they were fighting against sleep.

I can't. Naomi thought. *I can't commit such a sin. What had Anais done?* She wasn't sure she wanted to know. She dug her heels in and tilted her head back to look up at a sliver of crescent moon.

When she dropped her gaze back down, its eyes had slipped shut.

Dominic and Fortuna resumed their cigarettes and then looked at her expectantly.

"I can't."

Fortuna nodded towards the handsaw, frowned at her. "It sleeps now. You do it soon."

"I can't," Naomi repeated. She forced herself not to look at the trailer. To give any indication she'd talked to the boy. She didn't want to get him into trouble. "I cannot. And you—you shouldn't do this. You should let it go."

Fortuna raised her eyebrows and shrugged. "Hmph. You must not like so much being mother."

Naomi swallowed down a burning rage that made her eyes water. "She will get well without . . . that."

Fortuna snapped at Dominic in her rapid-fire mystery language.

He shrugged and threw up his hands. Then pointed at Naomi and said more, sprinkling "Damien" throughout.

He turned to Naomi. "Fine." He shrugged. "Come. I walk you back to the car."

"Poor child," Fortuna lamented, shaking her head.

~ ~ ~

Naomi looked up at the stars as she followed him back. She could see them better here than in their city apartment. *I should take Sam camping. Somewhere to see the stars.* She hadn't done enough fun things with her. She had taken her to see shows on ice and to the ballet. But they should go out into nature more. Sam had loved the petting zoo. She loved animals.

"Put the blindfold back on," Dominic said sharply when they got back in the car. Naomi felt the tears wet the material right away. "Don't take it off. Hope you know this will cost you more," he added savagely.

Please, she thought. It was times like this she wished she had a rosary. *Please remember the number. Please call me. Please let's make it happen.*

Early in the morning, Naomi drank coffee and tried to clear her mind from the lingering effects of the Xanax. Despite the pill, she hadn't slept. All it had done was add a layer of grogginess to her alarmed state of mind. She gazed out at the headlights still on in the dark morning traffic through the window. She knew Anais was an early riser. She texted:

"What did you do?"

"Don't ask."

"How can you live with it?"

"I have Lukas."

Naomi didn't reply.

~ ~ ~

She made sure her phone was charged and the volume up. She prayed. A few minutes later an unfamiliar number was calling. She crossed her fingers, heart thudding.

"Fortuna left, Dominic is asleep. Probably back in a couple hours so if you want to bring her, do it now."

"Where are you?"

He gave her the address.

Samantha was not a morning child. She complained sleepily, as Naomi bundled her into warm clothes and handed her a breakfast bar. "You said no appointments today, Mommy."

"We are going somewhere different. It's a surprise. You can sleep in the car if you want to."

The morning was foggy but lighter out now. The air was soft and slightly warmer as they got into the car. Naomi punched the address into her phone. It was thirty minutes away but could have been two minutes or an hour from the way she felt.

"Where are we going, Mommy?" Sam asked sleepily.

"Shh. Sam, you'll see."

Sam dozed in the car. Forever fatigued and foggy from medication.

After she parked, she clutched Sam's hand as they made their way past the first couple of trailers. An old man smoking a cigarette sitting on an overturned block of cement playing fetch with a dog. Two tired looking women bustling off in maid uniforms. And Naomi and Sam with their air of having come from a different world.

The boy met her halfway down the path. At least he wore a flannel now over his shirt. She could see him better in this morning light. He looked different. Even younger. Just a child too. Tall and thin, with large features and the same pale blue eyes as Dominic. She doubted he was eighteen. "Come on, I'm trying to wake her up more. She's still groggy from the nectar. I don't think she can help if she's not awake." He looked down at Sam with a prompt curiosity. "Hi," he smiled.

Sleepy as she was, she was aware enough to be shy and hid behind Naomi.

"Come on."

They approached the kennel. Sam gasped, the whites of her eyes—still sickly yellow—grew wide. Her mouth dropped open and she looked back and forth from Naomi to the creature in the kennel.

The boy made a little crooning noise and stuck a sprig of rosemary through the bars to rub against the unicorn's face.

It blinked and opened its eyes to look only at Sam.

The little girl took a step closer, entranced. Naomi sucked in her breath.

The creature hobbled a bit forward and dipped its head down so that the tip of the horn rested for a moment in the space between the little girl's eyes. Then it touched her on the lips. A light appeared, sharp and piercing, like a spark of electricity. It made Naomi and the boy flinch back, but Sam didn't move. And then it was gone.

"Okay." The boy reached his hand through and stroked its cheek and said something playfully in that other language. He turned to Naomi and Sam. "You should go," he looked around furtively.

"Thank you," Naomi whispered. "What about you?"

"What about me?"

"What will you do?"

He grinned. "I'm out of here soon. Going to stay in the city with my cousin next month. I will get a job and have a phone and never see Dominic and Fortuna again."

"What about her?" She tilted her head toward the kennel.

"I'll do my best. Need to call my cousin. If he can bring his truck, we can get her out before they get back."

Sam blinked. The unicorn slumped back into the cage. The little girl turned up to her mother. "Why do they keep it in a cage? It should be in a meadow."

Before Naomi could answer, the door slapped open and they heard a shout. Dominic came around the corner, shirtless, in slippers, his face taking everything in in a moment. He started shouting at all of them. The boy stood before Naomi and shouted something back. Then he turned to them, "Go. Now. I will deal with him."

Naomi bustled off with Dominic shouting obscenities at her.

Sam, frightened, started crying.

In the car ride they were quiet and Naomi put on Sam's favorite pop music. They both sniffled and for a few minutes they didn't say anything, both of them shaken, wanting to put distance between themselves and that place.

When they turned onto a familiar freeway, she glanced back at Sam in the rearview mirror. Her daughter's eyes were clearer than they'd ever been and there was a healthy flush to her cheeks. She looked more alert and awake than ever. "Sam?" Naomi said softly.

Her daughter blinked and met her eyes in the mirror. "I feel . . . really good, Mom." Naomi registered that she'd addressed her as "Mom" instead of "Mommy."

Naomi smiled. "That's why I brought you there."

"What will happen to it?" Sam bit her lip.

"I don't know, sweetie. That boy is trying to help it—to get it out of there and away from those people."

Sam sat up straighter. "We should go back. Go back and help him save it. We could find a meadow to take it to."

"Not right now. It's too dangerous."

Sam shifted her gaze to stare out her window. "I knew you'd say that. She needs people like me and him. We are young and we aren't afraid." The words echoed in Naomi's mind like a chant.

When they got home her daughter pointedly took her pill bottles and tossed them into the trash. Then Sam went into her room and closed the door.

A couple of days passed and when Naomi tried the number on the phone, she hung up quickly when Fortuna answered. Later, she drove there, by herself. She was nervous, but the trailer, barn, and kennel were all gone. She stood in the spot where the kennel had been and turned in a circle. She walked around the edge of the property. In a patch of wet dirt she saw hoof prints. Naomi leaned in closer and saw they seemed to glitter. She followed them a few yards into the trees until the shadows in the bracken darkened her path and then she stared off into the trees, wishing for a sharp moment that she was young. That she was not afraid.

LACUNA MISPLACED

by

R. TIM MORRIS

I kill the engine at the top of the parking garage, the old, towering one that overlooks a darkened Manhattan from Brooklyn's crumbling coastline. You're already there with a coffee for me and a still-hot pizza from Spadowski's, inviting me over, not with words spoken, but simply by opening the grease-stained box. You place the box on the hood of the car and we take a seat on either side of it. The pizza smells fantastic, sweet almost. This car hood, however—the engine already cooling in the winter chill—is freezing my ass off.

I motion toward a seemingly empty spot atop the steaming pizza. That slice there . . . it's missing a piece of pepperoni.

You ask, *Is it missing if it was never there to begin with?* Then you take a slice from the box, folding it in half, the melted cheese now cradling the grease rather than merely acting as a slippery platter.

She did that too.

She was always bragging about her preference for Chicago deep dish pizza, but then I'd inevitably catch her cramming the thin, bi-folded slice into her mouth, eating it like an honest-to-God real New Yorker.

She deceived me. Like the distance between the earth and the moon and the moon and the stars, she was deceptive. I have memories of her, but the memories are only fluid; it's the dreams that are concrete.

You say, *That's backwards though, isn't it? Aren't dreams meant to be the more elusive of the two?*

My dreams? They're like a bridge that spans over everything else in my cityscape, casting an unremitting shadow, while leaving me wondering just where exactly it is they connect to. A bridge you've seen a thousand times from below but have never stepped foot on either side. One side always being the end, I suppose, while the other will always be the beginning. It doesn't matter which direction you face; the two are always there. One cannot exist without the other: a symbiotic relationship. Beginning and end. Cheese and pepperoni. Her and me.

Oh, but that girl. That girl. I could see the end of us, even from way back at the beginning. The end was always there, like a traffic light in the far distance. A red light that never changes to green.

But that was then. This is now. I don't recall you agreeing to meet me at this place, but we're both here nevertheless. Why you asked me about her after all this time I have no idea. It's been months since it ended, but I guess you were just giving me my space. Or didn't want to share the space I've been in? Maybe that's more like it. I wouldn't blame you, really. I know I can be incorrigible at times. There's something about this squalid parking garage, too; it plays in my mind like one of those intangible memories. Its noxious blacktop stink sparks feelings I don't like having. The dusty, murky way its light and darkness play off one another, as though something here had done me wrong in the past. Whatever it could be though, I can't place it.

But maybe you had some entirely different reason for avoiding me until now.

Your space is your own. I wouldn't impose, you say.

She told me something about space too. She once described her being in my life as filling all the empty spaces within me. So why do I feel emptier now than I did before? Like she took a little extra from me when she left.

Lucky to have extra to give, I suppose? You wipe your mouth with your sleeve. Mechanically, you seize another piece of pizza and begin anew. I finally take a slice for myself. You know, sometimes I get going and forget the little things I want. That coffee smells good too. Thanks.

Our beginning was improbable. She, a young, ambitious art dealer who already had a half-paid mortgage on her own apartment in Morningside Heights. She wrote what she labeled "a popular column" for The New Criterion, some intellectual critical periodical I'd never heard of before. Me, I was nothing more than a struggling student who had no idea what I was supposed to be studying and, sometimes, no idea where I might be sleeping the next night. But she was the one who spoke first when we locked eyes on the subway. We had both—on a whim, it turned out—taken the 6-Train to Pelham Bay for no other reason than because neither of us had been there before. As it happened, the beach was terrible and the two of us bumped into one another, crestfallen while boarding the train back to

Manhattan. Purposefully, she sat beside me and started blabbing. "The heart wants what the heart wants, I suppose," is what she told me later when I'd asked her how it must have all happened; when I asked her why she would ever choose to strike up a conversation with a total stranger on the subway. She called it her opening move. Her gambit.

Does a gambit not imply that her move also included a sacrifice?

I suppose. If you want the proper definition.

What do you suppose it was she sacrificed?

I can't say, really. I dismiss you with a wave of my hand so I might continue. Later that evening, I say, after a lengthy meal at some expensive SoHo brasserie, we sat shoulder-to-shoulder out on the tip of one of those long Chelsea piers. There was a carousel glowing behind us, full of life—lights and laughter—on such a quiet night. It was then when I actually started to believe this could be something. Something meaningful, like the way a relationship was supposed to be. It certainly wasn't my first relationship, so I must have felt the same way before, but I couldn't recall. It doesn't matter either, I guess.

It was also then that we spotted something skipping across the Hudson. A light, like an engorged firefly, darted in and out and in-between our senses. We saw it and we felt it. We relished it and we didn't. At once, we prized it and also resisted it. I know it sounds stupid but that light—that will-o'-the-wisp or whatever it may have been—disappeared inside of us. We absorbed it in a microsecond. Each of us knew the other had experienced the same phenomenon, but neither wanted to speak of it.

Whatever it was that we'd experienced, it was strange enough and weird enough that acknowledging it was out of the question. Even to that person sitting right next to you the whole time.

And I was acutely aware that something else had entered the relationship then, too. Some third party completely unknown to us.

You mumble something with your mouth stuffed. I don't catch it though. You've already consumed a third piece of pizza, and you greedily reach for another.

She was the first thing I would think about upon waking. When I looked in the mirror she was there. Like any relationship, I suppose. Before we're too jaded to take them seriously anymore. It's what we were like before we'd been burned one too many times. Or burned ourselves, seems closer to the truth.

But then things end, don't they? It's inevitable. Not all at once, of course. That would be too easy. And it would hurt a lot less.

You say, *If it doesn't hurt it doesn't count, right?*

Sure. Like I said: the end was always right there laid out before us. It was no secret. It never is. She had a breakdown one night about some older brother she'd never mentioned before and how he molested her when they were kids. It happened just like that: right out of left field. After that, I don't think we had an evening that didn't include some amount of tears in it somewhere. She admitted to wanting to be someone else because anyone else wouldn't be her. I joked, "You're crazy! Everything you are is perfect." And then she seemed to take my joke literally. The *being crazy* part, that is. Through more tears, she blatantly informed me I wasn't motivated enough to lose weight. I didn't know I needed to lose weight. She accused me of the stupidest things; everything from swiping five bucks from her drawer to leaving a paper bag of dog turd on her doorstep and even hating minorities. Seemingly at random, she would become verbally abusive towards waiters and baristas and doormen.

I was desperately grasping at straws. I wasn't sure where things had taken this turn or how to fix them. Eventually, I spoke with one of her gallerist pals to figure out if her current state of mind was in any way normal for her. Is she like this when she's working? Is she bipolar? I was expecting him to inform me that yes, she would frequently stop by to intentionally splatter wine on the paintings, or maybe throttle the neck of a potential buyer. But he suggested to me—and quite bluntly—that perhaps I should seek help. Maybe I was the crazy one in the relationship. I recall this colorful painting of a field on the gallery wall. Every time I glanced at it though, it appeared to be a picture of something else. For a tiny moment I considered the possibility that the man might have been right.

It was soon after when we finally reached that red light. When it ended. We'd gone for a walk together and wound up sitting on that same Chelsea Pier. The carousel had been closed for maintenance. We didn't know what to do with ourselves and I suggested we return to Pelham Bay. But I didn't propose the idea as a last-ditch attempt at resuscitating the relationship. The one thing that might have gotten us off life support. I just said it. I said, "Let's go. Put on your best dress and we'll hop on the 6-Train."

"I don't want to go back there," she said. "That beach was terrible. I hated it there."

"But that's where we met!"

"Exactly," she said brazenly. Not a tear in her eyes. I think it was the first time in a long time that we'd spent the night together without any tears.

You ask, *And that was that, wasn't it?* I'm curious to know how you could tell, and you only say that's how the end always comes. *There are never tears at the very end. If there were, it wouldn't be over yet.*

I've never noticed that before. Maybe I just hadn't paused long enough to think about it. And it was also then—as she and I at once exhaled what we had left inside of us—that the light left. That strange, scuttling thing expunged itself, though we didn't immediately notice. Then, when she turned to leave, I saw the entity, or whatever it may have been, skipping across the Hudson River once more, this time heading somewhere far away from me. Maybe back to wherever it came from in the first place. She must have sensed its disappearance eventually, but the two of us never spoke again after that. Not of supernatural occurrences and not to each other. I still don't know what it was that happened.

What did you do with yourself once it was over between you?

What have I been up to? Just coping, really. There are still too many bad thoughts, too many illogical words rattling around inside my head. I want to say I hate her but I hardly even knew her. How can you hate someone you barely know?

I drink a lot. And there's too many bars around here to ever get too emotional about things. One weekend, I finally did return to Pelham Bay.

Was it as bad as you remember it being?

It was worse, actually. But I didn't meet any psychotics on my way back this time around, so there's that I suppose. Did you know there's a place called Throggs Neck out there? I had no idea. That must be the strangest name ever.

I finish off my coffee in nearly one gulp, and I realize there's only a single slice of pizza left now, too. I met someone new the other day, though neither of us are really that into each other. I dropped out of college but I do have a regular place to sleep now. You take the last piece of pizza without even asking, and then unconcernedly toss the empty box from the parking lot rooftop.

Listen, if you don't replace some of those negative thoughts with a positive one or two, they'll never go away. You must remember some of the good things about her?

If pressed, I might say her hair was orange like the perfect sunset. She appreciated opening credits in movies; the order in which they appeared and how they might be presented; fonts and that sort of thing. She once told me that love gives meaning to the stars, which I don't actually understand but it made a lot of sense at the same time. I really liked that.

You told me she deceived you. Do you still think so?

She wasn't the person I thought her to be. Is that enough to qualify?

Are any of us, really? Maybe you were only mistaken. Perhaps she didn't do any of those terrible things.

Then it's obvious she's deceived you, too. You wipe your mouth with your sleeve again as I consider the idea of perceived deception. What supernatural element decides whether a relationship will end amicably or in anger? Why do we seem to conveniently forget about the good times? I don't know if whatever she did to me would have happened regardless of whether we met or not, but I still find myself questioning my own sanity at times. I search myself for some truth to it all; some certainty that I'm still somewhat in control of who I am. That I have some say in my hopes and fears and heartaches.

I catch the light out of the corner of my eye; I see it just as it floats effortlessly off the rooftop. And when I turn to ask if you saw it too, if you caught this maybe-wonderful/maybe-portentous thing skipping away into the distance, you're nowhere to be found.

SHORT CHANGED

by

ELOISE ARCHER

On a west facing street, nestled beneath the overhanging awning of an apartment building, sits a phone booth that is fluent in the entire history of human emotion. Though its skeleton fades into slate surroundings, every summer marigolds bloom at its feet through the cracked pavement, and each morning birds perch upon its shoulders in neat, even rows. Creatures seem to seek it out—not by sight but by the tug of a rubber band that creeps back onto itself, settling into the same grooves once more.

Each member of the town felt this inexplicable pull, like an umbilical cord, or a noose, and would often find themself staring at the booth from their home; the plexiglass walls flexing in the winter wind under their gaze. An adornment of small holes severing its midsection served as windows, the hull of a ship giving the outside world a glimpse into its callers' journeys; rain staining waves against its sides.

Each land has its own lore, its own rhythm, but we often forget the ways of our ancestors; their fears, their gods, their love. So, in order to reconnect, the earth has to do what any good parent does: communicate to us in a language we understand, an olive branch gently rapping against our window panes in the night. Some say that's what the phone booth was; a reminder of whose land this really belonged to, a connection to the old ways. There are many places on earth which fall into each other until they travel somewhere else entirely; somewhere old and vast, with flickering lights. There are also hours where the world before us dips its fingers through the veil as if testing the waters, reminding us of obligations as siblings often do and whispering, "She's our mother too, mind your place." Many people experience this sensation as shadows that seem to swallow the light, or driving past a new diner on a lone road, where the patrons seem too still to be human, too stiff to be anything more than cutouts.

There were people who'd claimed they'd received calls from loved ones from beyond the grave; messages of them saying goodbye. No one could explain them, but 'sophisticated folk' wrote them off as a Connection Delay. The phone company blamed a crossed wire here, an electrical interference there, "It takes a while, sometimes, for the voices to get through the line." It became a superstition, as things in small towns often do. Ladies would gather around their kitchen tables and speak of dead husbands who'd called in the middle of the night and made them feel like girls again. Snippets of conversations with the deceased passed amongst barley sugars and tea so hot it made their teeth twinge.

Coins slowly found their way inside hems and brushing, ever gently, along socks inside steel-toed boots. The town folk would make their way to their jobs, each interaction moving the next into place; and inside their pockets the coins would click together in a Morse code prayer. Their clinks would blend in with the pitter of their footsteps and the patter of the rain and the whir of machinery until the air itself was music and the sun, quite hideous, looked down on them from the sky.

With lore comes rules and consequently a list was made on double spaced, blue lined paper, in the home of one Anne Kreline, and taped to the inside of the phone booth's walls.

1. A deceased individual can only speak with the living via the phone booth; no other known modes of communication share this ability.

2. Conversation is only possible if the deceased has the correct amount of change on them at their time of death, not a cent less.

3. Only one call per deceased is able to be made and as no details are given of the afterlife it is assumed the booth is located in a state of limbo.

4. Calls from the dead can be made years after their death with them believing only moments have passed as time works differently for them.

5. *Never dial the dead.* Never, under absolutely any circumstances, is anyone to dial the number of a deceased individual from the phone booth. Households with one phone for multiple people can still be contacted from the booth as usual as long as the *intent* is to speak to a living person.

6. All individuals now deceased are to be crossed out of the phonebook with their name added to a Do Not Call list located inside its front cover. If the number of the deceased belongs to a household where other individuals are still living, an asterisk is to be placed beside it with the dead family

member's name in order to avoid accidentally dialling the number with the intent of speaking with them.

A pen connected by a long string to a support pole also made its home in the booth, sitting next to the thick slab of a phonebook as a makeshift sceptre, a self-appointed warden of the dead. There is a great appeal in places without judgment; the equalisation of grand emotions. That's the power of it; a confessional. You are expected to fall, at least occasionally, to pieces in this church not built from piousness or reverence, but from the complete and utter appeal of transparent breakdown—this holy place, this man-made relic, this church of dial tone hymns.

As technology grew and advanced, the citizens of the makeshift church remained loyal because they felt the connection to the booth the same way sailors feel the sea in their bones; distance never dulling the gnaw of an oncoming storm. So when they passed each other they'd nod though rarely speaking, "We're the same, you and I", they'd think. "Our fingerprints have overlapped so many times that I feel you in my bones, you've crawled inside me. I ache when you ache." Places have a memory. After years of being cradled to a cheek, tears pouring into its mouth, the phone booth knew loss and tragedy, three in the morning drunkenness, two in the afternoon alcohol anonymous help lines, the number of the most sought-after babysitter in an eight-block radius. It knew all of these things. Superstition used to say that cameras captured souls, but phones—phones capture moments; they capture lives.

Offerings were still laid at the booth's feet but as older generations passed more and more wrote the rules off as wives' tales and many became too busy for something as silly as belief. Despite this, the children still felt that strange pull because when you grow up somewhere it takes root in you like a seed. Their bodies, though smaller than their parents', were not laden with the practical worry of adulthood and so they had more room for a faith that was now so frequently brushed aside.

If rivers are a town's veins, then the phone booth was its heart, wrapped within a ribcage of steel and concrete that slowly, but surely, grew round it. Every road poured was a new calcification, every waste-site a new clot; the business of man-made paradise built on the backs of others. Places have memories, flesh. So they would build and the ground would spoil. They'd landscape prosperity and the plants would rot; the water would sour just a little more each time. So they would take from the earth and the earth would take from them in return. When you put enough energy into a place it works its way into the soil, until the ground bleeds red dirt; putrid sweet in thick muddy puddles, run through with tire marks that look like a crime scene. At night as the far too old and far too young lay in their beds they listened to the wet exhale of exhaust pipes on the highway; congestion sticking to the roadside like tar in the town's lungs. "She's dying", they'd think, "we keep sticking her with needles and painting her face; we've stretched her too far."

Then, with the sun would come the anticipation of penance; rays of daylight sweeping away regrets like a broomstick. The scent of sassafras would permeate the air as children tossed their hair over their shoulders to sling backpacks and book bags for school. Grandparents watching from the balcony as they ran below reminded them not to lose the coins in their pockets as the steam from thick soup danced with cigar smoke around them. The grandparents with fingers so yellow they were orange, rubbed red when it rained from massaging arthritic limbs. The grandparents who were told by their own children to keep their superstitions to themselves, that the modern world had outgrown them. It is funny, in a very sad way, how age calls even the most logical things into question.

So one rainy night, let's call it a Thursday, let's call it anything, a pair of brown suede shoes walked a soggy young man into the booth's arms and as he exhaled, the small fibres which made him unique left a film on the fogged plastic walls. A flyer for violin lessons rustled to thank him for his donation and it seemed as though it would go as it normally did; with the forming and speaking of words by one person and the reply of the other on the end of the line. Only tonight that did not happen.

Tonight, Erik Moreno walked into the phone both and dialled the number of his mother who had died a full three months prior. The phone booth, not wanting to deny the request of a parishioner, was slightly shaken by this turn, coins jostling amongst cobwebs with worry. Her name, after all had been added to the appropriate list. The number which she shared had all relevant information placed beside it in the regulation pen.

Still, the line rang, as phone lines are want to do. Why wouldn't it? He hadn't disconnected the landline—couldn't stand the judgment of the rotary staring back at him when he contemplated it. The cord kinked in all the wrong places from where she'd wrapped it around her finger while she gossiped, stretching the wires. She always said it would never need replacing, some things are fine the way they are; no point changing something just to be disappointed. No need to do anything at all really. So the phone rang, and in its ringing Erik allowed himself to believe that she would answer. That the apartment he now solely occupied would be lit up with the electric current of conversation; that the room would feel alive again. He got so caught up in thinking this that he didn't notice at first when it rang out. Until it was all he could notice. The dial tone echoed and swam circles around itself, gurgling through the receiver like sludge down a drain.

As the coins rolled back into the collection slot he slid, in tandem, to the floor, and began to choke; slowly at first, then louder and more violently until his body wracked with convulsions. Florescent lights flickering in tune with his pulse. There is a point which people reach when they realise someone they love, very dearly, is never going to come home again, and at that point they will find that they cannot cry no matter how much they try to because there is simply nothing left inside of them which has not crawled its way out.

The rules, rewritten dozens of times over the years on every surface of the booth, stared up at Erik from the concrete floor. A rhinoceros beetle marched ever onward across the fifth commandment: *Never dial the dead.*

Erik knew this, but knowing and believing are two very different forms of faith and neither made a man smart. Desperate times call for desperate measures. He didn't have a choice. His mother had slipped; fallen off her chair in the shower. No coins. Died without the things she'd lugged around in her pocket for decades. Died with an outstretched hand, turned cold and stiff on the tiled floor. The eyes go first, he'd discovered. They lose their colour. He'd found her lying there with glassy, wrong eyes; pathetic little grey things pressing against the sockets. Grey as the ocean; neck bulging on the side from her spine trying to punch its way out of her. No coins though. It didn't work if you didn't have them on you when you died. He'd tried stuffing some in between her fingers, thought that maybe no one would know. But it didn't work. No more calls from mother. No more clinking of the ever-present coins in her pockets as she walked down the hall. She'd even sewn some into the lining of her dressing gown. The rhinoceros beetle blinked. You're not supposed to call the dead, it's against the rules. He knew this, he was sure he did. What did it matter, anyway? What does anything, really?

The phone rang.

Erik lunged.

From where it hung, dangling and unhooked, it spun ever so slightly and immediately upon being touched stopped ringing.

Silence.

Breathing.

Electricity.

It is no small thing, to lend your voice to a device for years; it would be foolish to think you left no residue behind.

He knew that breathing; *that wet rake.*

He held the receiver tighter; his bottom lip pressed so close to it that it was almost touching. "Hello." When did his voice become so loud? he thought. Was that him? Had he spoken?

A crackle.

"Margery said it's her son's birthday next week." *That voice.* It was hers . . . it was hers but it seemed stretched somehow, the vowels hanging where they usually clipped.

"You remember him, don't you?"

He remembered this.

"He always wanted to play with you when you were younger and you wouldn't put up with it. You'd just sit there and cry all the time."

They'd had this conversation a few months earlier; her pauses in all the same places, and though this time he didn't respond it seemed to make no difference.

"I said I'd bring him something and I need cream from the store. Don't forget the cream."

His sight tunnel-visioned to his shoes, the brown suede ones, now wet from walking in the rain. Having tried to climb a nearby leaf, the rhinoceros beetle had fallen from the top and lay squirming on his back, trying to make his world right side up.

"I need the whipping kind, not that thin stuff. It's not real cream they sell you, it's white water. It's not real cream at all. They put paint thinners in the ice cream, you know? They're trying to bleach you from the inside out. They're trying to take you away from me until you don't look like your own mother anymore."

Erik tipped the creature onto his feet, shell so black it was blue.

"You remember that, don't you? You remember Margery? Her son used to cry all the time, pathetic little thing."

He'd bought three bottles and she'd poured them all down the drain.

She'd said they'd gone bad. He'd found her trying to pull the wiring from the wall, nails torn to the quip, saying the rats had ruined the fridge's cooling system. They were trying to sabotage her, she was sure of it.

"What's taking you so long?"

The voice, her voice, crackled as hissing filled the line, static so silver he could almost feel the sparks on his skin. He thought about how he used to press his hands against the television when he was little and she'd fallen asleep in her chair; his palms pressed against the salt and pepper snow. He used to think it was magic. When he held his breath and watched the dust zap against the screen he used to think it was magic, these tiny weather systems in the wires.

"Erik?"

He used to think a lot of things. Now, he didn't know what to do with the armchair, nor the half-empty bottles of sauce in the fridge—her half bottles of sauce—nor the last of the half-eaten meals she'd hidden in the freezer behind the corn, or the thick pieces of chocolate cake now hard as rocks, scarred with imprints of her dentures.

"Riky, where are you?"

No.

"Riky! I'm scared!"

Not this.

"You're not in your room, and someone's broken in."

Anything but this.

"They've moved all the furniture around. Ricky, they've taken all the photos and I can't find your father."

There was that choking noise again, clawing its way out of his throat—

"Don't tell me to calm down!"

—knocking his uvula against the soft palate.

"What is this? Riky, what's happening?"

She wouldn't let him in the front door at first until he'd shown her his licence. She kept saying that her Riky was only a boy, wasn't anywhere near his age. The neighbours had come in after she'd kept screaming his name, screaming for help. Mr. Lane from next door had almost smashed his head in with a frypan before he'd realised what was happening. Riky had thrown all the knives into a shoebox later that night and hidden it in the back of his closet, stomach souring and rolling against his insides.

Passing headlights threw the booth into technicolour, rain blurring his surroundings. There was a hesitation, the slight hitching of breath, and then finally he spoke.

"Mum?" Erik's voice came out thicker than he'd intended, wet in all the wrong places.

The phone booth *shivered*; there is a reason for all rules.

Laughter crawled its way across the line and into his ear.

"You've been drinking, Riky; I can hear it in your voice. I ought to wring your neck, you know that?"

This isn't what he'd wanted. This wasn't her, not the way she should be.

"I ought to wrap my fingers round your throat until I milk it out of you."

All these echoes, all these regrets, he'd just wanted to say goodbye. He wasn't content with what he'd been given and now he was only left with dredged up bad memories because the good weren't his to give.

"You've got a skin full; it's sweating out your pores like molasses."

There was that choking again, that awful sound living in his throat.

"Your insides are rotten because I let you have too much sun when you were small. Now you've pickled them."

He'd broken the rules. You weren't supposed to call the dead because when people die they leave a version of themselves behind for you to remember, but if you won't remain content with what they have given you, if you try to disturb them, then you will only be able to think of your regrets.

"You've pickled them and they're swimming around each other."

If you're not careful, you can spend your life grasping to the past; listening to echoes of everything that went wrong until your love gets so thick you choke on it.

"One day you're gonna open your mouth and your lungs gonna fall out."

The rhinoceros beetle crawled out of the booth's threshold and beneath a nearby streetlight. His feet lifted high into the air causing him to stagger slightly. Erik knew this wasn't her. It was her voice, sure, the conversations they'd shared, but it was just a memory. The beautiful thing about memories is that they can be shuffled in and out of each other until all that remains is the good if you are willing to leave the bad ones behind. He stood. The creases in his pants rearranged themselves to a more appropriate appearance. His shoes, the brown suede ones, had left the patches of rain on them to fade into mere shadows. He lifted the receiver, such a small thing, really, and placed it back onto the cradle. Some of the most difficult things in life to do are merely a series of movements following each other with a determined resignation.

The rain had gentled and wet his hair only slightly as Erik stepped out of the booth and began making his way home. He nodded to the rhinoceros beetle, now asleep, suede scuffing against the pavement. As he walked he looked up towards the sky, at the shoes thrown across telephone wires, hanging themselves with their own laces. He looked at a town retracing its own steps until they begin again, chasing its own tail; always going forward but always, always stepping back. He swore he felt a thrum, the exhale of electricity beneath his feet.

CIRRUS

by

ISANA SKEETE

Job stops his run when he notices a pen on the ground. It's nice, a shiny blue fountain with silver filigree detail and it bothers him to see it lying in the middle of the pavement so he picks it up.

There's a boy standing in the grass a few feet away watching him. He doesn't look like the kind of person to carry a fountain pen: university-aged wearing frayed jeans, a washed-out blue t-shirt, and sandals. It's fifteen degrees Celsius out but he doesn't seem cold. Though who was Job to judge when he wears long sleeves in twenty-five degrees.

"Hey," Job says, "Is this yours?"

The boy doesn't respond, just continues staring. Job looks behind him but there's nothing there, just the cars parked on the opposite side of the otherwise empty road, street lights still on in the early dawn. Nothing interesting at least.

"Hey," he calls again, "Is this pen yours?"

The boy looks startled and swivels around frantically before he seems to register that they're the only two in the park. "You mean me?" he asks, pointing to himself.

Job frowns. The kid looks terrified and it sets all kinds of alarms ringing in his head. There's definitely a market out there for pale, huge-eyed, wisp-thin boys. That would explain the rundown clothes and that accent. Was it something Eastern European? Job's shit at sorting accents out. "Are you okay? Do you need help?"

The boy shakes his head. His expression calms down a bit, the tension in his body lessening. "I'm fine. I mean—I'm sorry. I was distracted by the street."

The boy's voice is soft, words disappearing into the puffs of breath. The relaxed version of a runner trying to speak after a sprint. It's the voice Job imagines a cloud would have. One of those cirrus clouds all high in the sky where there's not enough oxygen.

Job chooses to believe the boy and his current body language. He feels kind of shitty about it, but he has work in an hour. "Is this yours?" He waves the pen.

The boy shakes his head. Job nods, but now he's unsure of what to do with the pen. He doesn't want to put it back on the pavement, but taking it is probably a kind of theft and there's someone watching him, so he doesn't want to look like the type of person that steals.

"You can probably take it," the boy says, "I don't think the girl who dropped it is coming back for it."

Job slips the pen into a pocket, still feeling a bit like a thief but at the same time feeling compelled to give the lost pen a home. "If you saw her drop it, why didn't you tell her?"

The boy stays quiet for a while. "I forgot, I guess." He smiles with every part of his face.

Job is caught off guard by the gentle joy of it but he returns the gesture, conscious of the mechanical feel of his facial muscles.

"You should continue running," the boy says. "It's getting late." He points to the horizon where the morning sun is easing over. Job checks his watch. It's almost ten past six and he has to be at the hospital for seven. When he raises his head, the boy is gone. Job looks around, but he doesn't see any sign of him. He reaches into his pocket and feels the pen for validation that the encounter happened at all and he decides the boy must be very fast.

~ ~ ~

Job yawns as he slips through the door of the flat after work, flicking on the light and toeing off his shoes. He places them in their designated space on the bottom row of the shoe rack then stares at the two pairs of bedroom slippers on the top rack. His hand hovers over his usual with smiling cats printed on the front.

"Which pair is mine?" Job asked as Saúl took them out of the shopping bag. Saúl grinned, holding the cat pair out to him. "You're definitely a cat."

Job takes down the other pair, the one with dogs, and slips them on. He doesn't want to feel like a cat today.

The mail is lying on the table. He looks through it as he shuffles into the kitchen then tosses it onto the counter. Bills. A "Something for you" card from the post office.

He fills a glass under the sink and looks in the fridge for something to eat. There's milk but he doesn't feel like cereal or oats. Maybe a sandwich but that's not appetizing either. The longer he stares the less he wants to eat. He sighs, closing the door. He notices the sheet of paper in front of him then, small heart-shaped magnets on the edges attaching it to the fridge.

'I'll pick up my stuff tomorrow – Saúl'

Job slides off the magnets and folds the paper neatly before dropping it into the bin.

It's time to sleep.

~ ~ ~

Job has the day off so he meets Xavier and Adiella for an early dinner at their usual Italian in Soho. The waiter shows them to a table and places the menus in front of them. Xavier orders a bottle of wine.

"You look like shit," Adiella says.

Xavier agrees and Job shrugs.

"By the way, we're just going to sit here until you tell us what's happening," Xavier says.

Job grimaces and brings his hands up to rub over his face. "Saúl and I broke up."

"Again?" Adiella says. Xavier glares at her across the table.

He had been avoiding this conversation because of this scepticism. "Well, it's over this time," Job says, face still covered. "He moved out and he's living with Ferdinand now."

"So he leaves you for some side boy toy?" Xavier presses.

"He didn't leave me. It was mutual. It wasn't working so it didn't make sense struggling when we were both unhappy," Job says, ignoring the implication that Saúl would have cheated on him. That is one thing he's sure of. Saúl isn't that type of person.

"So he said, 'Let's break up,' and you said, 'Ok,' because Saúl always knows best." Adiella gestures to continue but looks over to Xavier and stops.

"No. Yes, he said it first, but it felt like all we did was fight lately." Job doesn't add that he had expected Saúl to come back like always, not to move in with Ferdinand, not to forget how good they were when they were good.

"Jo, both of us know how much you love him, as close to unhealthy emotional dependency as it is," Adiella says.

"Adsy, I'm not dependent"—Job seethes the word— "on Saúl."

"Jo," Adiella says, "we've been here through your arguments and break-ups and make-ups, so we know how much it all affects you. I mean, I, personally, am not upset to hear that Saúl is finally gone for good and"—a cough from Xavier interrupts her— "we just want you to know that we're here for you."

Job sighs, pinching the top of his nose bridge to relieve the beginning pressure of a headache. "I know. I know. Thanks." He feels everything but thankful.

~ ~ ~

The door is open when he gets home. He checks his watch. It's already seven. He thought Saúl would have been done by now. The dog slippers are missing from the rack.

He takes off his shoes and leans against the wall. Maybe he had a bit too much wine.

"So you're like a dog then?" Job stroked Saúl's head like he would a puppy.
"I guess so," Saúl replied. He licked Job's cheek and laughed.

Job steps onto the floor in his socks, nearly slips. Now this would be a dramatic time to pass. Would Saúl cry for him?

Ferdinand is standing outside the bedroom. Resentment takes hold of Job and he hates that man more than anyone he's ever spent the energy to hate. He's not exactly sure how he's supposed to treat the man who's stolen his boyfriend but he doesn't think he needs to be courteous.

"You always did make a shit blond," Job says.

Ferdinand frowns at him, running his hand through his bleached hair. "Saúl likes it enough." His broad mouth reveals too much teeth and gum with a satisfied sneer as the sourness of Job's expression deepens.

Saúl comes out of the bedroom and eyes the two of them suspiciously. Job feels a bit queasy from having to stand in his flat with his ex (fuck Saúl for doing this to him) and his ex's new plaything (there's no way Saúl is serious about a flaky guy like Ferdinand). Saúl passes off the box he's carrying to Ferdinand and tells him that he'll meet him downstairs. Ferdinand tries to kiss him before he leaves but Saúl stops him. Job hopes Ferdinand falls going down the stairs.

"I really thought we could work it out, you know," Saúl says.

Job stays silent, stares determinedly over Saúl's shoulder at nothing in particular. Out of the corner of his eye, he can't help notice the way Saúl's shoulder-length hair hangs to the side, in that cultivated layered mess that makes him look too much of a model. Did he lighten it? It's got that summer sun highlight like that time they spent two weeks in Miami. All water and sand and the spray of a rainbow constellation of stars peeking out from the top of too short swim shorts. Job closes his eyes and breathes out harshly.

Saúl sighs. "Jo, I tried. We tried. It didn't work."

Saúl's voice is pleading, as though he thinks that's enough for Job to forgive him. Job wants to kiss him or hit him, maybe both, though he's not sure of the order.

"And him," Job says pointing to the door, meaning Ferdinand. The gall to bring him inside this place, their place. "He had nothing to do with it. It had nothing to do with the fact that you were fucking Ferdinand." Words are coming out of his mouth without his brain's approval, but he can't take them back. They feel justified, just for the hurt they cause.

"I already told you," Saúl says, evenly without any sign of indignation. "Nothing ever happened with Ferdinand while we were together. This has nothing to do with Ferdinand. This"—he waves his hands broadly drawing the flat, and so their years spent together here, into his words—"was broken before I even met him."

"Are you done?" Job says, catching Saúl's gaze. Saúl's disappointment shows in his brown eyes, so glossy they remind Job of a tiger's eye gemstone or a cockroach's lost wing. "See, we can't even have a proper conversation. Fuck, Jo." Saúl crosses the distance between them and kisses Job's cheek. "I love you but we're better off like this."

Job thinks he hears Saúl's voice crack but he ignores it. Has to ignore it. He closes his eyes again and tries to pretend that Saúl isn't there; that this isn't the last time he'll hear Saúl speak his name or feel his breath against his skin. Job only opens his eyes when he hears the front door close. He takes the cat slippers from the shoe rack and shoves them to the bottom of the garbage.

~ ~ ~

It takes Job two weeks to accept that he can't stay in the flat. No matter he tells himself that it was his. Saúl had moved in with him, not the other way around. But they still turned this into *their* flat. The couch they got off Gumtree for fifty quid with the cushions that Saúl had re-stuffed and re-covered so that they no longer matched the rest of the fabric. The bed from an actual shop, though the shop owner was Job's aunt's patient's cousin and the bed was overstock from the previous year and had come with a wonky leg. Saúl had a carpenter friend from down at the theatre fix it for the reasonable price of dinner and a few bottles of prosecco. This all was supposed to be temporary anyway. Saúl wanted kids and had this dream of raising them in a house in Dulwich that, to Job, was more reasonably Bromley since Job didn't fancy being beholden to Saúl's parents. They had fought about that. Saúl hadn't understood why Job wouldn't want his racist parents' money. 'They'll get over it when they realize this is for the long-term.' Well, they hadn't and it turned out that they knew their son better than Job thought he had.

It takes Job two weeks to find a new flat.

~ ~ ~

New Cross to Clapham seems like an appropriate distance. He sells the furniture for less than he probably should and buys a few pieces from Ikea for their reasonably priced simplicity, gets them delivered because the only person with a car (who he doesn't mind asking for help) is Adsy, and she drives a Fiat.

Even though she can't help transport anything, Adsy comes over to help when the Ikea furniture is delivered. Xavier works that Saturday and if the angry emojis in the group chat are anything to go by, he's miffed to miss this "transition to a purer space" (™ Xavier Tiné).

He and Adsy spend most of the day building everything. The mattress is straightforward and the bed frame isn't too bad to put together. But then they spill the small parts for the chairs and it really should be easier to find a one-inch screw, but it isn't when the flat is full of boxes and packaging.

The flat is a second-floor one-bedroom and within walking distance of the station, which makes it easy to get to London Bridge for work. It's also across from a small park. Job appreciates that it's got some trees and even flowers as well as a children's playground. A nicer view than just the flats across the road.

He goes down to the park when Adsy has gone home and the natural evening light begins to cast long shadows across the makeshift football pitch in the park where four little boys are kicking a ball about. The space of the outside helps him forget that the flat is smaller than the one in New Cross and that everything smells new. He wanted to move and now it feels wrong to have abandoned what was once a sacred place. There wasn't that comfort of going home to someone you love. Despite the fighting, there had still been joy and beauty between them. Now he just had sterile walls and makeshift furniture.

There are benches behind some trees where he can observe the entire park. Best to make use of the late light now that the city was truly well on its way to summer, to when he could enjoy a sufficiently warm bed with only one body before winter skids round and leaves him missing the familiar heat of another person near him. He's lost in his thoughts and doesn't notice the boy sitting on the bench until he's about to take a seat. The dark mussed up hair is familiar as are the large matching, sleepy-looking eyes underneath. Job is certain that the ripped jeans and threadbare t-shirt are the same as the last time Job saw him. He's unsure whether to sit and acknowledge the kid or move to another bench. He takes too long to make a decision and the boy looks up at him.

"Fancy seeing you here," Job says and has to physically resist the urge to cringe as he realizes that it sounds like a creepy pick-up line.

The boy's forehead, understandably, furrows in confusion. "You keep seeing me." His voice is still breathy, this time like it's cold and he's trying not to let the heat out; quick words, barely opened mouth.

Job wonders what language would influence that strange sentence. Asking would probably increase whatever depth of creepy he has to now climb out of.

"Can I sit here?" Job says as non-threateningly as a six-foot black man can be to a pale waifish very early twenty-something. He feels like he can't ignore the kid now that he's acknowledged him.

"You shouldn't talk to me," the boy says.

Job steps back reflexively at the firmness of the statement. It sounds very much like something someone would train a child to say to strangers. But this "boy" definitely isn't a ten-year-old.

"No!" The boy shouts suddenly holding out his palm to stop Job from moving.

Job freezes, wondering if this is going to turn into some sort of fucked-up situation where he gets accused of trying to solicit in a park frequented by children. Clapham is starting to look like a bad idea.

"I didn't mean that you couldn't sit here. I just meant that talking to me is a bad idea." The boy bites his lip hard then releases it, red from the pressure.

It's cute, Job thinks, and then reels in his mind before it can dive any deeper. His mind always tries to do this: think what it doesn't need to think. At least he catches it this time. Sometimes he forgets and then he's trying to imagine what it would be like to tie Ferdinand up and then . . . things he doesn't want to be thinking about.

"I should probably go," Job says. He lifts his hand to look at his watch, anything to fake lateness to a non-existent engagement. "It's getting late."

Job doesn't wait for acknowledgement of his statement. He turns to leave before the exchange can get any more bizarre.

The children playing football have stopped and are staring at Job. Anyone would want to know what was happening with the shouting and Job hovering in front of a confused looking young man. Job gives them a small smile to try and show that everything is ok. The children scatter, taking up the bottles they were using as goalposts and darting across the park.

~ ~ ~

Tuesday and Job hates chance meetings. First that odd kid in the park and now he's staring at Saúl inside the much too small Northern Line train as the doors close. If this is punishment for forgetting his work laptop at home, he thinks it's a bit excessive. The only thing that would salvage the situation is pretending they hadn't seen each other and riding south in feigned anonymity. But this is Saúl, who manages to look too gorgeous with his messy bun and paint-stained dungarees, not a person with common sense and courtesy. Saúl smiles at Job gently, like Job's a pitiable injured toddler, and moves around two men taking up too much space with their conversation about the best prawn pappardelle to stand near Job.

"Hey," Job says first. Dogs can smell fear.

"Hey. Deli has some fabric down at the haberdashery in Tooting, but she has a tutoring session so she can't pick it up," Saúl says, as though Job gives a shit about the heartless puppetry of the universe forcing him to spend fifteen minutes on the tube with his ex.

Job nods.

"How are you, Jo?"

"Fine," Job says. He's baffled that Saúl thinks it's all right to call him "Jo" like he's family or a close friend. He returns the question, spits it like a scared cobra.

Saúl lets out a breath that could be a laugh. "I'm really glad to hear that you're well. You always forget to take care of yourself when you're upset, but you look good. I'm not too bad myself actually, even if Deli likes to be unreasonable, like I'm not just volunteering to help paint the sets." Saúl's expression softens, a cautious puppy happiness. "Thanks for asking."

Job hates the agreeable air of it all. It's so genuine and Saúl's smile is bright. He's pleased to see Job. A month later and all Job can do is rein in the scowl wanting to spill onto his face. He feels like he's only getting more upset with each day, and he has no idea when he'll feel the reverse.

There's a delay at Stockwell so the trip is closer to twenty minutes. Saúl talks the entire time. He's going to miss the students in the Fine Arts Foundation course. They've had an extra layer of enthusiasm that the BA students don't necessarily have. One of the MA students punched a hole in her thesis and he and the senior technician, Rachel had to play counsellors as she bawled. Job eventually stops trying to pay too much attention to what Saúl is saying. He finds himself listening to the Spanish inflections in his English. They're stronger than usual. He'd probably gone to visit his family in Mallorca over the weekend. Job always liked the way the Spanish would bleed into the English so slightly. The accent to the English words around *querido* when he tried to say it as Spanish as possible because he knew it turned Job on. It disappoints Job when they slow down at Clapham South because he knows this won't end with a kiss, with the knowledge that they'll see each other later.

He exits the train and becomes frustrated that Saúl didn't seem bothered being near him. That reminds him to be upset.

~ ~ ~

It's been weeks, but Saúl stays on Job's mind. He's trying his best to maintain that Saúl's casual conversation is unreasonable, but keeps wondering whether he's the one being unreasonable for feeling hurt after two months. It's hard to focus when he's anxious about losing the righteousness of his frustration. He takes the bus home more often, avoiding Saúl trumps getting home quickly, until he gets sick of thinking about that meeting on the Northern Line every single time.

He almost turns to the bus stop, but decides to get home quickly and open that bottle of cava he still has from Xavier's housewarming gift.

The cava finishes too quickly to effectively stave off the loneliness he's been avoiding for the past weeks. It's still early enough that the Londis on the corner is open. He grabs a bottle of the sole chilled white and some crisps. It's bad to drink on an empty stomach after all, and he may have started badly, but he could finish while attempting to right that.

There's someone sitting in front of his door when he climbs the stairs. He approaches slowly and realizes it's the boy from the park. The hair, the jeans are the same as the past two times. He stands when he notices Job.

"You see me now," the boy says smiling. "I'm sorry. I know I went about the last time entirely wrong." He looks down demurely, waiting for Job to forgive or reject. He sneaks a look up and their eyes meet.

Job has no reason to not accept his apology. It seems genuine enough, softly spoken with an apologetic look. "Yeah. No problem, but how did you know I lived here?"

"Of course, I saw," the boy says.

It doesn't make sense to Job, but this kid is so confident in the answer that Job manages to rationalize it in his mind. He must have seen Job from below and figured out which flat it was. The answer was probably just a language barrier thing.

"What's your name then?" If he's going to be seeing him around, it would probably be best to put a name to the mess of hair and doe eyes.

The boy looks pleased to be asked, but his expression becomes confused for a moment. "I'm not sure how to translate my name."

Another very strange idea. Job's not exactly sure why he would want to translate his name but Job's ready to put in the work to say it properly. "You don't have to translate it; you probably shouldn't translate it. It's your name, isn't it?"

The boy thinks very seriously, eyes unfocused and mouth pursed unflatteringly, though there's something nice about him allowing Job to see a face like that.

"I guess it would be something like 'The bud of God that is the second shell of fellowship.' "

There's a moment of silence as Job squints bewildered at this kid who looks satisfied with his "translation."

"I can't really call you that though," Job says, as hesitantly as possible to avoid the possibility of sounding like an asshole.

The boy deflates into his thinking face again. Job waits, stifling impatience. Why did every conversation with this kid go as smoothly as crunchy American peanut butter? Just when he's starting to get annoyed instead of just puzzled, there's a clap of hands and an excited face. They look nothing alike, but it still makes Job think of Saúl in the middle of a painting that's going well. That moment after Job has just dragged him from the studio and is trying to pile him full of the food that he's forgotten to eat that day. A grateful joy. It's the way his eyes crinkle at the sides as he grins. Job's breath catches in his throat at the prettiness of it and he almost misses the name.

"Yehavkiel. That's the closest I could come up with."

"y-AAV-keel." Job says it slowly and knows he's probably said it wrong.

Yehavkiel nods. "Ok!"

"Did I say it correctly?"

"Sure."

It sounds as though Yehavkiel is just accepting Job's terrible pronunciation out of some happiness that he was in the general vicinity. Job doesn't think he'd ever accept anyone calling him "j-o-b" instead of "j-OH-b" but it might be just as rude to insist that someone pronounce their name a thousand times just because his mouth couldn't comply.

They stand there for a few seconds, Job unsure what to say to Yehavkiel's beaming face.

"Um—Thanks for the apology and letting me ruin your name." Job moves toward his door and pats Yehavkiel's shoulder as he passes.

"You touched me." Yehavkiel somehow breathes out the shout.

Shit.

"Fuck. I'm sorry. I forget some people don't like to be touched and—" Job stops when Yehavkiel takes his hand, turning it over and running his fingers over Job's palm.

"Please don't apologize. I was only surprised." Yehavkiel's look of wonder is disconcerting, but Job thinks he would feel awful if he pulled away and caused that look to disappear.

Fingers trace lightly up the underside of Job's forearm. He's surprised at the way it makes him shudder. Not just a tickle. The kind of shudder that Saúl previously had monopoly on.

Yehavkiel grips Job's hand in both of his and squeezes. He's trembling slightly as he looks up into Job's eyes. His pale face is dusted with pink and a somehow innocent sultriness. "I—" A pause. "Can you touch me more?"

Job can't look away. He tries but he can't move. He attempts to speak but what is he supposed to say?

"It doesn't have to be much, just—just a little bit."

To say that it's the oddest way Job's ever been propositioned is an understatement.

There's a small weight resting on Job's chest and a softness on his cheek. It pulls him up out of a deep slumber. He blinks his eyes open in time to see a face, Yehavkiel's face, dissolve into a glittering dust.

~ ~ ~

Job wakes up alone. The other side of the bed is cold. He forces himself out of bed so he can go pee. The last time he'd woken up alone after sex was the morning after he lost his virginity, but he had never thought he would wake up alone after taking someone else's. It would have been a very awkward morning, but he had been prepared for that. Now he has nowhere to channel his awkward preparation. He laughs sleepily.

Job passes through the kitchen for a glass of water, taking in the silence of the flat. The white wine is still in its bag in the kitchen as he passes to the front door to replace the safety chain into its latch before he showers for work.

He stares at the door. He finds himself turning around to the window behind the small dining table to ensure he's still on the second floor. He realizes he's being silly and he turns back to the door, shakes the chain expecting it to fall off somehow. When it doesn't, he opens the door. The opening is still only wide enough for a very lean cat. He's walked through the entire flat since waking up and there's not anywhere with space to hide a whole adult. He walks back to the bedroom confused but deftly avoiding any concrete thoughts.

"Yehavkiel?" he says into the emptiness. There's no answer. Not that he expected one. Just really hoped.

The bedside table catches Job's eye. The fancy fountain pen he had found lies on the pad of paper he had tested it on that first day. He picks up the pen, turns it around in his hands to feel the realness of it, before he pops off the top. Powder pours out of the cap and he manages to catch some in his palm. It's all-coloured and dazzling like crushed precious stones, like a dream come true.

UNEVEN AFTER THE BREAK

by

CHET SANDBERG

I walk to the door and say it three times. "I'm sorry. I'm sorry. I'm sorry."

It won't work if I don't say it aloud—might not work even then, but it's too much to face without a magic spell, and what's the point of a spell that doesn't work?

I dreamt about her again for the first time in weeks. Her voice is the same as it ever was, the same as I remember. People say memory fades and becomes untrustworthy over time, but that's not true for everything, and especially not true for the hard things.

Out in the hall, the carpet muffles my steps, and the dirty yellow light casts envious rays on the offensively inoffensive beige eggshell of the wall. The crooked lines of carelessly accumulated white enamel on the baseboard molding collects dirt that seems to be painted into it. I bend and run my fingers along it like a child might, and now my finger is dirty, but the dirt on the molding isn't lessened at all.

The stairwell takes me down to the street-level door, then I'm out. I'm not sure I'm really awake, but she can't throw me from a high place if I stay as low as I can.

The keys in my pocket press into my leg, and I reach to reposition them as I step under a streetlight. It's 3 a.m. and I don't need to be out, but when I open my cigarette box to light one, there are only two left. I spin the lighter's wheel and scratch a flame into existence just long enough to get the cherry started, then deeply inhale the pinched wrongness of Camel Menthol Lights.

No one is out tonight as I approach the convenience store lot. In the squat building, under bright lights on the other side of the window, soundlessly, the clerk leans back, away from the counter.

Probably not dreaming.

I take another drag, then look at my cigarette, nearly finished. I nod, because I didn't feel it, but time passed and I must have been lost along the way. I let go and step on the butt when it lands, even though there isn't anything flammable for miles.

Ding-ding! as I enter the store. The clerk told me his name, more than once, but I don't remember and I feel I've used up the number of allowable asks to not be considered rude. Funny I should feel that—funny I'm alive to care about a clerk who thinks I'm inconsiderate. These weird worries are all that's left after the passing of too many key life events and wrong choices have melted the colorful world into a grey soup.

"Hey, Steve," the clerk says.

I smile. "Hey, man."

The clerk narrows his eyes. "You doing okay?"

I take too long to answer, which means no matter what I say, the answer is no, so I'm left searching for the correct shade of *no* to keep us both disentangled on the surface of a friendly relationship that isn't a friendship.

He saves me. "That bad, eh?"

I swallow, but before I can say anything, he says, "You look—" He takes a deep breath and there's curiosity behind his eyes.

This is a shockingly intimate moment, the sort of moment that sometimes happens in the early morning under angry fluorescent lights, but I'm still not sure I'm awake. Does he know?

The clerk doesn't finish his thought, so I say, "Yeah, man," and shake my head, and the unbearable camaraderie lifts. I'm free of the two-man conspiracy against sleep deprivation or madness, or whatever it was he wanted us to beat.

He backs up, and the way the light falls against his nametag brings my attention to it. It plainly reads 'Jeff'.

"I need a pack of cigarettes, uh . . ." I'm torn between using his name or not, because maybe he saw that I had to look at his tag, and in my head, the entire vignette of his disappointment plays out, and I can't bear it—I decide I don't have the emotional resources for it, even though I'm still not sure I'm not—at this very moment—sleeping in my bed on the fifth floor of my complex. "Uh, Camel Menthol Lights?"

He nods and retrieves the cigarettes from their perch in a display above the counter. "That it?"

I nod.

"Ten sixty-seven, Steve."

I fumble for my wallet, then drop my card on the dirty blue-grey tile. When I stand after picking it up, something in the air has changed, but I still want my cigarettes. Jeff points to the card reader and I reach to slide the magnetic strip, but Jeff grabs my hand and I freeze.

His voice has changed, and it's her voice. "You should have gone through with it, you coward."

I want to move, but I can't.

~ ~ ~

Winter, 1995, in a small town in Michigan

We'd been fighting—we were always fighting because that's how love always is with me and there are things I can't feel properly except after fighting. I was sixteen and she's fifteen, and our families are crazy in a way that might be funny if it's not happening to you.

"Please stop doing this to me." The look in her eyes when she says it makes me want to die and I suggest as much.

There's quiet in the late night and it's snowing and she's wearing a cute fuzzy hat that somehow amplifies the sadness in her wet eyes. I can smell her, even in the cold, the way she smells—a combination of laundry soap and some fruity shampoo, and the tinge of cherry ChapStick—filters through the dry air and tickles the inside of my nose because I didn't smoke then. I didn't start smoking until . . .

"I don't—" I stop. She's leaving in a week. We've tried to make the best of it, to live and love as much as we could in the time we have left, but it's been a series of arguments about the dumbest things, and not always coming from my end.

Her father is drunk in a room somewhere; my mother is drunk at home. I'm sober tonight, like I'm sixty-five and all the color has been beaten out of me, because it has. Martin, her father, is leaving Mary, my mother, and though we've not been found out—which had been our greatest fear—the outcome is as dire. All our plans, all the money I've been saving to get us clear of the deep, frozen Midwest alcoholic trailer life momentum, all is for nothing and my two-hundred and eighteen dollars can't dig us out.

Her father's the more dangerous one, because of course he is, with his mechanic's hands the size of baseball gloves and his dark hair and dark eyes and dark threats of violence that always seem just shy of oozing out past whatever it is that keeps him just short of murder. There's a touch of that in his daughter, my love Sarah, but it hasn't eroded the better parts of her yet, and if I'm able, somehow, it never will.

I step toward her and she surprises me by stepping forward too, so now her five-foot-three-inch body is the entirety of my existence, which is exactly enough for me to believe in the rightness of the world with zero remainder. "You can ask my mom."

I feel her tense up. Sarah's never gotten along with my mother. Neither have I, but blood keeps us tied together like crippled dogs and will for many years until she dies, appropriately, of cancer in 2018.

"It's three more years, maybe only two if I can get work and we can—"

"Okay." Her voice is muffled where her mouth is pressed against my chest, so it vibrates my ribcage over my heart. She's never agreed to this before, and I worry it'll be dreadful for her, that maybe it'll let her father's sickness in further and wash away the angelic light in her eyes that makes me want to console her and fuck her at the same time in the most confusing teenage way.

I step back and I think I may have started crying. I nod and my breath is quick. "We can. After she's sober"—I step back—"no, after she's only had a couple. She always starts out happy." I think of my mother then, and her pinched, mean face in the half-light of the living room, shrouded in smoke, and I say a prayer to a God I'm certain can't exist. Please let us get out of this place.

It's three nights later, and Sarah and I are in the kitchen with my mother, and she's drinking vodka. Starting with vodka means there'll be terror later, but it means she's loose and mostly smiling, and the teasing is good-natured. Martin is 'working late' in the shop, which might mean he's passed out drunk in a corner or truly putting the pieces of a customer's truck back together.

"You guys are"—my mother sips from the vodka—"you'd make a good couple, if you weren't brother and sister."

Sarah gives me a look and my heart stops, but mom doesn't notice. "We're not related, though."

Mary shrugs and says, "I guess not." She gets an odd look in her eyes. "I don't know why I thought of that just now."

I try to be casual, and I shrug, but maybe too emphatically. "We're around the same age, I guess."

Mom looks at us across the messy, cluttered table. Cigarette burns have pockmarked the thick plastic of its surface, creating ridges. I nervously scratch at the uneven ridges. When I look up again, mom's eyes are glassy and she's looking through us, like there's something on the wall. "I'd say I'll miss you, but . . . he's gotta go." She nods solemnly at Sarah, then at me.

"You know . . ." I begin tentatively, because here's where it could be blown, "Sarah's doing really well in school here, and she's made a lot of friends. It's not fair that she's gotta move halfway across the country just because you and Martin are over."

Mom startles, and an honest-to-god look of empathy crosses the normally hard, wrinkled surface of her face. She sighs. "I know. But . . ." She lets the thought drift and pours herself another vodka and Squirt.

"Mary?" Sarah asks.

"Huh?" mom says.

"Is there any way in the world . . ." Sarah sighs and a pained look crosses her face. It's clear she's conflicted at the thought of asking for this, that she knows my mother isn't kind and that she sees Sarah as some sort of competition, despite the vast chasm of years between their respective ages. "Could I?"

Mom's face is blank; the vodka has slowed the speed at which thoughts traverse her synaptic spaces. Then her expression softens again, and for the second time in such a short time, clear signs of empathy shine from her glassy eyes. "Dear"—she reaches across the table for Sarah's hand—"what are you asking?"

"Could I just . . . stay here?" Sarah shifts on her feet.

Mom rocks back in her chair. My mother thinks of people in terms of their functions and roles in her life, and it's clear she's never considered Sarah much of anything but a bit of flotsam attached to the man she wanted to love her. "We don't make a lot of—"

"She'll be sixteen in June. If she got a job?" I suggest.

Mom sighs. "What does your dad think about this?"

Sarah winces. "I . . ."

Mom smiles and nods. "You haven't asked him yet."

The room is silent as the smoke from mom's cigarette floats over everyone. A half-open door on the cupboard over the sink draws my attention, and I zone out. I swallow hard when I force myself to be present, to be back in this room.

"Don't you think you should do that first?" my mother asks.

"Yeah. Yeah, of course." Sarah looks down and shakes her head, then looks up again. "But if he says okay?"

My mom narrows one eye. "I'll think about it."

~ ~ ~

It's a day later. I'm waiting for Sarah to come back from asking her dad about staying. I'm in my room, trying not to be nervous and failing.

The door creeps open and I see her blonde hair first, but when she looks up, her eyes are ringed with red. She's been crying.

Oh no . . . "Honey?" I open my arms and she runs to me.

She's not sobbing, instead only making quiet sniffing noises against my sweater in the space between my chest and my armpit. She looks up. "He thinks it's about a boy."

My breath catches in my chest before I realize she means some unknown boy, and out of all context and despite the roiling septic tank of my uneasy emotions, I'm shocked that Martin understands—to some extent—his daughter. I feel intensely naked, as though it's possible to easily see straight through me, and also through her.

"He doesn't think it's *you*," Sarah says.

I nod, and she looks up because I didn't realize she couldn't see me; that's how locked in my head I am. Can I convince Martin without giving us up, and what would be his reaction to that?

I lock the door so no one walks in on me comforting her. She looks at me and she's not crying anymore. She pulls up my shirt.

~ ~ ~

Martin is in his shop and weirdly not dead-drunk. For the first time this week, I wonder how he's taking the split with my mom. For me, she's a constant negative stimulus, something from which to grow away, but Martin slept with her for years, and though I'm new to sex and Sarah was my first, I can't imagine he could go that long without finding something lovely in her. The bizarre insight seems to come from without, from the air or like the solution to a perplexing algebra problem I didn't even realize I'd taken in.

Martin catches me unawares. "What the fuck are you doing here?"

He's right. Everyone my mom has been with has a preternatural skill with machines and I lack both the skill and the interest and always have. *A boy who doesn't like trucks or guns, how weird.* But I'm here and his eyes are narrow, so I'm guessing he knows it's on behalf of Sarah.

I take a deep breath.

He doesn't let me start. "She's not staying with that bitch just because she's into some boy. I don't care what you say, I'm not letting your mom screw her up the way she's fucked *you* up."

I try not to smile. The total lack of self-awareness is something I've already seen in so many of the people who inhabit the orbit of my social class. *We're not screwed up, never us.*

I cock my head and fold my arms in front of my chest. "She's doing well here, man. Let her finish out high school here. She's made friends."

Martin violently pulls the cigarette from his mouth and drops the shop rag he'd been holding. "She can make friends in Alabama."

When he brings it up, my heart breaks and I can't hide it. I blink rapidly to hold back the tears. It's so far away. "Alabama . . ." I'd known, but it's like I've heard it for the first time.

He nods. "Family there, yeah." He cocks his head and his eyes go wide because I'm struggling with every inch of strength within me to not break down, but I'm failing. He gasps. "Oh my god." An evil grin creeps onto his face. "It's you. You little motherfucker." He picks up a wrench and maneuvers around the car he's working on as he comes toward me.

I put my hands up and back away and he throws it—throws it wide, thank God—and it clatters first against the aluminum wall, then the concrete floor. He's still running. I turn and dash out the door into the night.

"You've done it, you little fucker!" he yells. "Better say your goodbyes, because we're leaving tonight!"

My crying slows me down, but I don't stop running.

~ ~ ~

She shoves the pill bottle into my hand. "Take them. As soon as I can get to a phone, we do it. Together."

Were I to look back on this moment, and look back I will, it seems like such a stupid idea, but when you're young and in love like we were in love, the idea that we might meet again in a few years is inconceivable. Who would break the other's heart first? When I got home, she flew out the door with me and we ran to the abandoned shack where we first consummated our passion. It wasn't planned we'd be together the last time there, but it was fitting. We fucked like crazy, even though it was so cold now, and she shivered and I shivered, but it only felt like more of the energy and love we felt for one another.

And when it's done, that's when she hands me the pills.

I nod. I would fight dragons for this woman. We contemplated murdering Martin and my mother, but life in prison, separated forever, wouldn't be much different from what we had already considered. Surely, suicide was easier. Right?

I can barely breathe as she leaves the shack. We agreed she'd go alone, so as not to anger Martin. I wait an hour and cautiously start for home. When I get there, she and Martin are gone.

~ ~ ~

It's two nights later when Sarah calls me. She's crying.

"It's horrible and I miss you so much, and Dad has been awful and making fun of us the whole time," she says.

I take deep breaths. Martin told my mother, but she's been oddly silent and damned near maternal about the whole thing.

The timing works. My mom is at the bar celebrating Martin's departure, so I'm alone in my room on my own phone. "Are you alone?"

"Yeah. We're at my aunt's. Her and dad are passed out," she says.

There's a long pause on the line where neither of us dares say a word.

"Do you still have the pills?" she asks.

"Yeah . . ."

We each take twenty. The bottle says hydrocodone/APAP 10/325. She tells me they're Lortab. I'll learn later that the Tylenol—the APAP—was the more dangerous thing.

We talk while the pills kick in, going over our first kiss, the shared lust we kept hidden from one another for so long, how I was mean to her at first because it was too dangerous for me not to be. Our responses get slower. The last thing I remember before passing out is that I'm smiling and I feel warm.

I wake, and the phone is making a disconnected noise. I don't have her number. Trying to stand, I flop back after only rising an inch from my bed. My vision is blurry. I can't see the edge of my vision and I panic. *I'm going to die!* It hits me, hits hard, and I'm terrified. *This was a stupid plan! There was hope for us, what the fuck were we . . .*

I fumble with the phone, trying to remember who to call, then trying to focus on the numbers. 9 . . . 1 . . . 1 . . .

Someone answers, but I don't remember what she says. "I'm dying," I say.

I don't recall much else, but I try to get out as much as I can; I'm so scared and my brain won't cooperate. Only near the end do I remember Sarah.

"My girlfriend! She's . . . She took them too, and she's in—"

But I was talking over the operator and she finishes, "—will be there as soon as they can. Try to stay—"

Everything is black.

Whatever romantic notions I had of an afterlife have been obliterated by that event. There's nothing afterward, it's just a deep black hole from which nothing ever returns.

They pumped my stomach. That's what they do, along with I.V. fluids, and I have to drink some terrible liquid that smells like rotten eggs because of all the Tylenol I had. I feel like death, but I now know it's better than death because I *can* feel this bad—because I can feel anything at all.

It's two days before I see my mother and another day before she dares tell me the news.

Sarah didn't chicken out.

The next two weeks are a numb gauntlet of shrinks and tests and pretending I'm okay before they let me out.

~ ~ ~

"You gotta pull the strip through it, man." The clerk examines me, probably wondering if I'm drunk or high.

I look at where I've frozen with my card at the reader and he's got his hand on mine trying to help me pull it through the machine. I recover and finish the transaction.

"You good?" the clerk—Jeff, his name is Jeff—asks. His voice isn't her voice and there's no condemnation.

I look at the liquor rack, then back at Jeff. It's been years since I drank, and though I didn't do a program or stand in front of people to tell them I'm an alcoholic, I recognize I had a problem.

My heart weighs eleven thousand pounds and I know that as deep as that dark hole of death is, I can't keep going on and I can't keep dreaming about her. No pills this time, not twenty-five years later. If it's pills, it'll just be another phone call and another hospital bill, and another twenty years of regret.

I'll need the booze or I won't be brave enough, so I reach for brandy because it was something Sarah and I'd had back in the day—stolen from my mother's liquor cabinet because she only kept brandy for when her father visited, and that was rare.

Nothing strange happens as I pay a second time. Jeff has a sad look on his face, like he knows he shouldn't sell me the booze, but it's not his job to refuse if I'm sober and old enough. I want to say something to him, to acknowledge his simple human-ness, because I felt it tonight and I'll never see him again. I don't, because the thought of him learning I'm dead and thinking back—I need to slip out quickly and quietly and fix the mistakes.

There have been so many. Samantha left me two months ago. The nightmares, the sleepwalking, she couldn't understand, and she sees I can do more than I do and wondered where the hidden strings were. I think she thought she could heal me, that she could or should be able to. As I leave the halo of the streetlight at the edge of the convenience store parking lot, I nod silently into the dark that it was my fault she thought that. It's always so hopeful in the beginning, and even I see it—that my eyes are bright and I can reflect so much vibrancy . . . it's easy to think my condition is temporary, and I want to believe it is, too. Of course, with every new face and the taste of each new set of lips, I think maybe there's hope.

But then Sarah shows up and she's so angry at me. She's in the mirror behind me when I've just had an orgasm and I'm cleaning up. She confronts me unexpectedly when I see my new lover sleeping and I fear she might be dead.

In a flurry of fast movements, I free the lid from the brandy bottle and I take my first drink. It's just sour fire, and I try not to gag. Why the fuck did I pick brandy? Anything else would have been easier. *Did you want easier?*

Touché.

I drink again, and again. Before I know it, I'm in my building, then on my floor. I pop into my apartment for a pad and pen, then dart back out, drinking more enthusiastically as I go. My blood has begun to ooze within the veins beneath my skin, and I feel like a much looser version of myself. I wonder why I ever wanted to get rid of this guy, but shake the thought away. There's damage that comes with it, and it can't be kept at bay by hopefulness.

Three flights up the stairs and I'm standing before the door to the roof. There's an alarm that goes off if you push on the lever, but it's so loose, you can lift it around the lock mechanism and get through. I stuff a dirty sock in the door jamb behind me—not because I'm going back, I tell myself, but because it's rude to not leave some sort of clues behind.

There's old snow on the roof because it's still late February. There's no light up here, but I've been here before. I light a cigarette and breathe it in deeply, satisfied it won't have the chance to kill me or lay me out in a hospital bed gasping for breath. I've been told not being able to breathe is the scariest sensation in the world, and that's why waterboarding works. I'm about to jump off a building, so I don't know why I'm worried about not breathing.

It all makes sense now—the nightmares about falling from a height or being thrown from a plane. I wake up every time in a sweat, but also feeling sick that I have to meet the new day.

I look over the edge and wonder about the lack of color. I gaze at the cherry of my cigarette and it's barely red, as if all the color has been drained from my life, and so it has. I drink again and see a shade of blue, the same as the sweater she wore under her coat. I pulled it off her so I could put my cold hands up her shirt that last night.

My eyes leak and I drink. My feet are getting numb, but it doesn't matter; they'll get me over the line—always have, and I've been numb a long time, I realize in a flash. I'm "dead with scenery," knocking out steps and heartbeats stubbornly because I'm the only one who doesn't know I've expired.

I drink more, and the weight lifts! The weight lifts further as I step to the edge. Don't look down. You'll bail out if you look down and you need this to end.

I regret the choice as soon as it's made, as my head gets too far in front of me for me to get back, but my feet haven't left the edge of the roof.

I'm falling, and I'm terrified, and it'll be over so soon.

And then I stop. My eyes are closed, so I can't see it, but there's a hand on my chest. The metronome I've become snaps back over as I'm pushed, and I collapse backward onto the roof, landing on my ass.

This is the part I can barely tell because no one would believe me. I wouldn't believe me. There before me is her face, and she's crying. She's so beautiful I can't breathe, and I'm stupefied. *Am I dead?*

I've heard her voice so many times throughout the years—in my dreams, in waking visions. I hear it again tonight.

"You need to stop. You're breaking my heart, and I can't stand watching you do this to yourself anymore," she says.

"What are you . . . How are you . . ." I saw the black on that night in '95, and I know there's nothing beyond it.

As though reading my mind, she says, "You go through the black, my love. And then through the light, but I couldn't." Her face is the same as it was, but her eyes look so much older. A tear drips from her eye; it hits my jeans and I shudder because it's so cold. I say nothing and she must be able to read that I'm confused. "You're still here, and you're not okay. I thought . . ." She turns away.

"I'm sorry . . ." I say.

"I thought Samantha would turn you around, but you're right back here again. Why are you back here again?"

"I'm sorry I freaked out and let you die alone." I've needed to tell her this for years.

"We all die alone. We were never going to die together. It doesn't work that way. If you died right now, we still wouldn't be together."

"I should've—"

"We were stupid, and now I'm stuck here, halfway between life and death, and I can't do it anymore. I need you to be okay. I need you to be *okay*." She looks nearly frantic now, and I'm blinking because I can't keep from crying. Another of her tears drips onto me, and again it's so cold I shudder.

"I wanted to—"

"If you kill yourself, I can't ever leave this . . . *in-between* place." Her eyes are hard. Angry. "I need you to move on. Your guilt is why I can't go. Don't you understand?"

I don't understand. Not a word. Not at first. "I miss you. I miss you so much."

Her face softens. "I miss you, too, but you have to stop. *I* took the pills. *I* killed myself. You didn't betray me, and if I'd been able to, I'd have saved myself before the end."

I'm still stunned. She picks up the brandy bottle and I watch as the liquor inside turns to sludge. She tosses the bottle over the edge behind her and a moment later, the sound of it breaking punctuates the night air. "You need to leave that behind, too. Promise me."

"I . . ."

"Promise me!" Her face is a rictus of fury.

"I . . . I promise," I stammer.

"*Call Samantha.* She thinks about you all the time, you fucking idiot."

Though I'm confused and terrified, I smile at that. I did love—*do* love—Samantha.

Sarah reaches out with her hand, and without thinking, I grab it. *Holy fuck, she's cold!* But I can't let go. She lets go when I'm standing and I shake my hand, trying desperately to get some heat and blood back into it.

"But what about the nightmares?" I ask. "And when you took over the clerk to tell me I was a coward?"

She stares, then flicks my forehead with a finger. "That was you. That's all you. I can't visit your dreams, and I sure as fuck can't possess people."

I want to speak, but I'm stunned again.

"Go. Get some sleep. When you wake up, you need to remember what I need. You need to move on with your life." She cocks her head. "Deal?"

I can't say anything. I swallow. She waits. After an eternity, I say, "I'll try."

She nods. "That's enough, because up till now, you haven't."

Now I nod. I turn back toward the door, and she follows me. When I crawl into my bed a few minutes later, she's still there. My eyes droop, and I lose her—truly lose her—forever.

~ ~ ~

In the morning, I wake. The memory of her is still with me, but I don't feel sick. I sit up, ready to start my day. Maybe I'll look for a job. I reach for my phone and freeze. A note in her beautiful handwriting is propped up next to my phone. "Call Samantha," it says.

I bring up Samantha in my contacts—I could never bring myself to delete her. While the phone rings, I think to myself, *I should get to know Jeff better. He seems like a solid person.*

Her voice comes alive on the other end of the line. "Hello?"

PERSEIDS

by

JUSTINE ROSENBERG

When September finally comes, they bundle their things into the trunk, leave the city with its electric halo behind, and drive out to the middle of nowhere. They stop when the highway turns to gravel. Sunny swings one leg out of the car. Her red heel bites into layers of crisp leaves and iron-dark earth. She listens to the roar of water curl between old trees, trying her best to think about glaciers and beetles and pine leaves. The sound of Paul shutting his door a little too hard startles her.

"There's a lot of stuff to carry in," he says. "Maybe just grab the drinks."

"There's no cell reception here."

"Yeah." He opens the boot, swings two green duffel bags over either shoulder, and looks sideways at her. "Jesus Christ, you're gonna wish you had taken a sweater. We're right by the river."

"Paul." Sunny yanks a tartan sack from underneath the back seat. The liquor bottles, crammed at strange angles inside, clink together. "Did you ever think that my mum might want to call me? Did that ever cross your mind?"

"Hey, I was just filling your requirements."

"My what?"

"When you said you wanted to leave town for a bit. No cell reception, lots of forest, somewhere wholesome. This is as wholesome as it gets, milady. The Internet told me."

Something hot and jagged sticks in her throat. "It's not even been two weeks since we buried George." The words stretch into the space between them. "She might still, you know, want to talk."

"Mum will be fine. Your sister's in the same building."

"Frieda? She fucking hated George. This is Christmas morning for her."

"And you liked him any better?" Paul shifts beneath the weight of the duffel bags. "First he was a drunk, then he was a junkie."

"And my mother is a psycho. They were perfect for each other." For a split second, George unfolds before her. He is dressed in a blue coat, having a cigarette in his favourite chair. He inhales comfortably. When he exhales, his face disappears behind swells of smoke. "We should've said something. There're government rehabs. There's counselling."

"He was no good for her, Sun."

Warmth spreads across her cheeks. She thinks of her father and the summer of his death, how her mother had vanished in the holes carved by his absence, resurrected in December when George arrived. "This vacation was a bad idea," she says.

"It was *your* bad idea, if I remember right."

Sunny tromps off, flattening clumps of dwarf mallow as she goes. She wants to turn around and hold Paul until his scent creeps under her skin, but the memory of George, slack-jawed beneath a white sheet, curves around her like a moat. She consoles herself instead with fragments of other years and other holidays, when she was barefoot and grinning for nothing.

~ ~ ~

At the end of the gravel lane, a carved sign stands in front of a big wooden house. *Welcome to Riverport Bed & Breakfast: Eco Retreat.* Webs of feathers and miniature wind chimes sway in front of the faded letters. "Hippies," Sunny mutters. She waits for Paul to check in. When he is finished, they make their way down the sawdust path.

"The owners are really nice," he says. "They've been doing this for, like, sixteen years. The wife says they used to run hiking tours and yoga classes before they got old."

"Hmm."

"What does 'hmm' mean?"

"It means 'hmm,' that's all."

When they arrive at their cabin, Sunny is disappointed to find that it is a tiny square with an outhouse attached. Her heels clatter against the stairs. When Paul unlocks the door, she shoves past him, drops her things, and throws herself onto the narrow bed. Beside her, the mattress dips and creaks.

"Sun." Paul's fingers are rigid when they touch her hair. "We'll be back in the city by Monday. Haven't you been talking about seeing the meteor shower for weeks?"

"Sometimes I just say things." She rolls over and looks at him. "I want to go home."

"There's no moon tonight. Won't be a better time." She watches the stiffness move from his fingers to his shoulders. "We get free breakfast tomorrow."

"It's vegan. I saw the menu online."

"It's free. We eat too much meat, anyway. Too many dead cows. Too much stress, too much noise. This will be great."

"I want a chicken burger." Sunny regrets the words the instant they fall from her lips. She has been meaning to say something pleasant to him for days. *I think vegan meals will be nice for a change, too.* Air stutters in her throat. Perhaps she has become incapable of pleasantries. "Guess we'll walk up the trail tonight," she manages. "You wanna bring the tequila?"

"Sure. Just stay off your ass long enough to actually see the shower."

"Paul." The image of George, face mottled and still, returns. Fentanyl, the neighbours had murmured, as he was carried from the building in his winding sheet. Perhaps they thought that speaking its name dispelled it. Pain blooms in her left temple. "Do you think he felt anything? I found the ambulance bills. He overdosed twice last month. She was asleep this time."

"Sun."

"She said his kids weren't gonna show for Thanksgiving. He had nobody but Mum. We should have been nicer to him, don't you think?"

Paul is quiet for a moment. When he lies down beside her, the leviathan at the bottom of her chest loosens its coils. All his night shifts at the port have made her forget the familiar roll of his limbs, adjusting and re-adjusting themselves. She puts a hand on his belly and pretends that August never happened. August is the border between asleep and awake. After the cheap grave marker had gone into the ground, Sunny shut her bedroom door, drew the curtains, and informed Paul of her decision to wait the autumn out.

Beyond the little window, tires crunch on stones. A car door slams. The sound of children shrieking at each other—*attends-moi, attends-moi!*—hits the fraying screen. Something between a grunt and a chuckle rumbles deep in Paul's chest. "Frenchies on our side of the country," he says.

"So?"

"Remember Mauritius?"

"Yeah." This time, she cannot help but smile. "That was fucking dumb."

"Was your idea. Can you imagine if we actually quit our jobs and went away for two years?"

"It just takes some planning. Tons of people are able to do it."

"Yeah, freaks and rich kids. We almost bought the plane tickets." Paul regards her for a long while. "The coffee shop called. Hilda said they're going to be short a bunch of people this month. She's asking if you're coming back or not."

"Tell her to stop calling."

"I think, maybe, if you just explained—"

"Tell her to fuck off."

He says nothing further. Sunny traces the crooked bridge of his nose. She almost says out loud what has been festering under her tongue: *It's not going to get better. Go find a girl who can hold down work. Go find a girl who doesn't spend all day locked inside. Go find a girl.*

"I love you," she says, and wonders at the same time what his mornings would look like with someone else. She pictures him at their kitchen table, chatting with a pretty blonde. His smile comes easily, like it did when he was unafraid of hitting the fault lines that have surfaced in her.

Paul works his fingers deep into the coarse mass of her hair. "We should get married," he says. "Sunny. Sunny Aronov."

"Sounds weird."

"Yeah." He yawns. "Long-ass drive. Wake me up in like, an hour and a half."

She waits until he starts to snore. Then, she presses a hand into his back where the slow, strong thump of his heart reverberates against the skin of her palm. Piece by piece, her mind builds pictures of her mother, mute in the silence of her ancient flat. *She will be holding the pillow where George would lay his grey-blonde head. She will have that look on her face, like a kid with a really hard math problem. She will have taken an extra Seroquel.*

Her eyes burn. She cries because she has full hands while her mother has empty ones, and because Paul is the captive of a woman with snakes for blood. These serpents must have uncoiled from between the legs of her family's first matriarch. For as long as she can remember, their fangs have dribbled an unnamed grief into the veins of her mother and grandmothers before. Shut-ins or suicides, all of them. Now, the patient snarl of cobras has overtaken her amid the carnage of George's death.

She knows that the end of autumn is a myth. She will remain asleep long after the leaves have fallen and grown back green.

~ ~ ~

It is dark when Sunny decides to go for a walk. A tide of frog song has burst the river bank and pierced the cedar walls. Her button-down shirt sticks to her back when she sits up. High heels clatter gently against the wooden planks.

"Be back," she whispers, but Paul continues to snore. She lifts the unopened bottle of tequila from its bag, pushes the interior lock down and shuts the door behind her. When the twilight prickles against her skin, she realises that she has left her key inside.

She takes her cell phone out of her pocket and swipes a thumb across its screen. No signal. She walks along the open ring of cabins, the spikes of her shoes disappearing into pits of sawdust with every step.

"Fucking clouds." Sunny stops at the big house that stands between the gravel driveway and the cabins. The owners are asleep. An exterior light peers out from beneath a battered awning, keeping watch over a garden patch. The trio of bars at the top of her screen remain hollow.

She wonders what Mum is doing right now. Probably watching some evening gameshow, the light of the television flickering over the vacant space on the couch beside her. Sunny knows that she is responsible for filling this space in whatever ways she can. It will be as it was when her father died. She will close ranks with her sister against the monsters that paw at their newly-lonesome parent, trying every synapse for a way in.

The familiar exhaustion gathers like pebbles in her lungs. She wonders if she should scream to rid herself of it. Only the sight of the vegetable garden, the shadows that lean against it, and the frog sounds beyond, quiet her. She puts the phone back in her pocket, takes off her shoes and uncaps the tequila. Body parts— little legs and wings—vibrate atop the wet soil. The dark smiles at her. Maybe this is where the dead go. Perhaps her mother is not so alone.

From somewhere behind her, a cabin door opens and closes. Sunny walks faster. The ground grows drenched and pliant. She imagines Paul waking up by himself. He will wander through their apartment and among her things: half-filled bookshelf, calendars bulging with forgotten appointments, stacks of foolscap inked with unfinished poems. He will be sad at first. But Paul is Paul, and eventually, he will extinguish her poison drop by drop. He will open the curtains to spring and its green harvest. This, she knows, is what he deserves.

Sunny thinks she hears her name. She stops only to tip the bottle against her mouth and guzzle the liquid from its neck. Throat burning, she clambers over a bed of rocks, feeling her way until she is mired ankle-deep in the silt of the riverbank. She drinks the bottle down to its label and says, "So, where are you now, George? Mum's been asking."

They have had this conversation many times before. He has never answered. At her mother's flat, Sunny was constantly on the lookout for doors closing by themselves, brittle-brown flowers unfurling overnight, mysterious noises in the walls. After three days with no results, she began to tell herself that George had become the tomato plant on the porch, or the birds nesting in a hole in the roof. Two days later, she came to realise that tomatoes and birds are no good when one is by herself in bed at night.

The clouds break, and the first thin tails of light streak the face of the river. The dark stops smiling. The forest is hungry, and Sunny is alone in the presence of beasts that watch her on four legs with lantern eyes. Each meteor illuminates the strange universe that widows and orphans are the sole navigators of. The weight of this kind of solitude makes her mouth go dry. She will have to bear it for her mother. She does not want to bear it for herself, as well.

High above, rocks jounce against each other. "Sun," Paul says. His voice drifts like fishing line towards her. She turns slowly and scrambles, bent almost double, halfway up the bank.

"I couldn't sleep," she says. When she holds out the bottle to him and he grasps it around the base, she feels the shadows retreat. "I didn't think it would start this soon."

"Thought you were in the kitchen." He takes a sip and looks at her. In the silence that follows, Sunny considers telling him, *Call Hilda. I'll come back to work next week. We could use some extra cash for our vacation fund. And while we're at it, why don't we let some light into that dungeon of a room?*

Instead, she says, "We'll need to find a good carpet cleaner for Mum. We can't leave his blood all over her floor. It's not good for her."

"When we get home." Paul speaks as if he is holding something between his teeth. He passes the bottle back to Sunny.

"I know." She takes a mouthful and sets it carefully between her feet. Another volley of light rakes the sky. Cosmic dust slithers between them. "You're right," she says. "We should get married."

"Sunny Aronov?"

"Yeah." Her face forms a smile. "I'm not kidding. When this mess is over, we should get rings for each other and stuff. It'll be good."

"Will it?"

"I'm sure."

"Sun, you're never sure."

Sunny does not answer him. They finish the tequila as the meteor shower streams by. She tries to keep track of the spears of light as they pass, looking for the places where they have left holes in the atmosphere. When the liquor makes her too dizzy to focus, she allows them all to coalesce into a flock of golden birds. Their glow obscures the shapes that hide in the dark. She thinks she might be swept away in their tailwind. Only the tug of Paul's silence keeps her in orbit.

When it is finished, they climb up the riverbank, fingers knotted together. Her naked toes leave dark smudges on the rocks below. She does not wonder where her shoes have gone.

MOUNTAIN VIEW CEMETERY

by
ABBY SIMPSON

Sometimes, it feels like all I've got left is you. These moments. I talk, and I believe you listen.

Maybe you can't. I don't know. Is there a time you're listening, and a time you're listening to someone—somewhere—else? I'm probably not the only one who needs you.

Deep down, I know you love me. Loved. I still talk about you in the present tense, as if you never left. Everyone says it isn't healthy. My therapist says I'm preventing the stages of grief from cycling properly. She says that's what's keeping me from accepting that you're gone. I don't know what she's talking about when she says it. I've grieved for you plenty.

What I do know is that when I sit in the cool grass, leaning against the extravagant black marble stone your parents etched with your name, your birthdate, and your date of death, I feel at home.

The bed we shared is a foreign object to me now. The springs feel like sleeping on nails singed with fire. I can't remember the last time I had more than an hour's sleep. Here, at the cemetery on the hill overlooking the North Shore Mountains in all their snow-capped splendour, I could sleep. This is peace.

But I don't want to miss you.

~ ~ ~

The call comes in at twenty-three minutes past midnight. I remember, because I look at the clock next to the bed and I scowl, like an entitled brat. You have a habit of calling me when you're out drinking with friends to tell me I'm the prettiest girl you'll ever know, to promise me favours in exchange for a grilled cheese sandwich when you get home. You like how I make it with sour cream and aged Havarti.

But this, though it's your number calling so late at night, is not that call.

"Hello. My name is Dr. Jyoti Singh. Are you Mrs. Lindsey Morton?"

"This is her," I say, sitting up in bed so quickly that the dogs are alarmed and jump up with me. They sleep on the floor when you're home, and we've agreed not to argue about the fact they sleep at my feet when you're not.

"Mrs. Morton, I'm so sorry. Your husband was in a car accident. He was brought in with a massive head injury. We did everything we could, but he passed away twenty minutes after the ambulance arrived."

My mind explodes, right then and there, as if there's nothing left to think about beyond the news I've just been given.

"No, it's not possible. I just saw him. Where is he?"

"He's still here, ma'am. Because it was an accident, the coroner will need to run a toxicology exam, and determine whether the blunt force trauma was what killed him. I'm so sorry for your loss."

I try not to get angry at the facts she's merely obligated to tell me. I'm a crisis counselor. I know how this works. But I don't believe it's real. This is a dream, and I'll wake up from it soon, with you next to me doing that weird half-snore you do when you come home drunk.

It's not real because you don't drive under the influence. We live in a city. With options. You never mind leaving your car somewhere, and going back to find it the next morning after grilling up every last strip of bacon in our fridge and pounding back the blackest cup of coffee.

This is a mistake, and Dr. Singh has it wrong.

Mistakes happen. I want to tell her she has the wrong man, but instead all I find myself doing is throwing on a pair of jeans from the laundry hamper. I don't even change out of my plaid flannel pyjama top. I don't think about the fact that I'm not wearing a bra.

I shove my feet into a pair of boots without bothering to find a pair of socks in the darkness. The dogs are looking at me strangely, their heads tilted sideways with round, sympathetic eyes watching my every move. They know nothing about this moment is normal. I can't wait to bring you home, safe and sound, and restore the balance. This will all be sorted by the time I get to the hospital.

~ ~ ~

That's you in the bed, head split wide open, skin black and blue, but I'll always know you by the freckle under your left eye, in the shape of a tiny Vancouver Island.

You grew up there, and you always say the freckle is proof the place would never leave you, but it's probably left you now.

The sum of all your life experience is lying, head split open, in that hospital bed. Your life with me, your parents, your stupid brothers that make you look like the Golden Child simply by existing. Everything you are is dead.

The rest of the night is a blur. I remember I can't stop crying. I can barely breathe, can't see clearly. My parents show up at the hospital, but I can't remember them saying a word. Someone tried to force me to eat a bag of potato chips, but I remember throwing up instead.

I remember there's a woman in the room next to yours. Dr. Singh said the two of you were brought in together. Same accident. Same car.

She's alive. I remember watching her, waiting for her to wake up. I have a million questions for her, because you can't answer any of them, anymore.

Why were you in the same car? Why didn't you tell me 'drinks with the guys' meant her, too?

Deep down, I know the answers already, but I can't leave the hospital without confirmation. By morning, she's awake. No family has come for her in the night, so when her eyes open, it's just me staring down at her. I don't feel bad. You've already been taken to the morgue, and my parents beg me to just go home, but I don't think they can understand how sincerely I feel like I have nothing left.

"I'm Bryce's wife," I say, and her eyes read fear, like she's been caught stealing, with her hand in the cookie jar. "Did you know about me?" I ask.

She nods.

"He's dead," I say. "The doctor said he was driving."

She looks away, her blonde hair a mottled mess of dried blood and machine wires. Her chart says her name is Jennifer, and my mind searches memory for any clues to her existence that I'd willfully overlooked. Tubes are coming out of practically every hole she's got, and though I want to throttle her, I know it won't do me any good. It won't make me feel any better.

"I'm sorry for your loss," I say. I'm parroting the doctors now, effectively on autopilot. Still, I barely manage to say it before hurrying out of the brightly-lit room and collapsing into the arms of my parents for comfort, in a way I haven't done since I was a lovesick preteen. Much as I want to let her hear it, it's you that I'm angry with.

The entire week after your death is a fog. I can vaguely recall being placed in cars and escorted to various places—the funeral home, the cemetery, our old bedroom—but I don't remember the process of living day to day. I just know that the only thing on my mind is you, and I'm constantly replaying the night at the hospital, meeting Jennifer, and how it felt that night like I lost you twice.

Your bills go unpaid, and I have to clear them since our finances are linked. I learn all about your second cell phone and your secret credit card, and piece together remnants of this other life you lived right under my nose, while I focused on eating right and exercise because we were talking about having a baby.

You left me alone to clean up after you, and I'm glad you're not here. I don't think I'd get through a moment without screaming.

~ ~ ~

At first, I don't notice I'm late. There's far too much else running through my mind. When I do notice, I know I'm not sick, so I assume I'm just stressed. Of course I'm stressed, but even after I've cleared our finances and sent most of your things to your parents' home in a U-Haul with your friend Jamie, I discover that you've left me with one more mess.

Our mess, as much as it hurts me to think about it, was wanted up to the minute I claimed your body that night at the hospital. The dream died with you, until it didn't.

I buy four pregnancy tests at the drug store because I want to be sure. Each a different brand. The girl at the checkout counter is young, and she looks at me like I'm about to ruin my life as she rings me through.

I consider that I might be. You left me with your debts, and with bad memories I never saw coming, and this baby will be a constant reminder of you.

Every stick comes out positive. I'm pregnant, and you'll never get a chance to be a part of it. I'm angry and devastated all at once for the fact you won't be here. I'm still not sure I want to do this. Not alone.

If only we hadn't waited for our careers to take off, to travel. Maybe we'd have done this sooner and you'd have been here. Maybe if we'd had a baby, there wouldn't have been a Jennifer.

But it's silly. We wanted our careers. We wanted to travel. We did everything exactly as we wanted to, as we said we would when we started dating our third year of college. The only moment I would trade is agreeing to give you a boys' night out the night you died, but I would have had no reason to. We'd have fought about it. And you'd have probably texted Jennifer when we retreated to separate floors of the house to cool off.

~ ~ ~

The baby is healthy and growing. I'm not finding out the sex, and I never imagined my mother would be my birthing partner, but the doctor says the only thing he's worried about is my mood.

I still think about what it would feel like, but I won't try to join you again. Not even after the baby's born. I understand that it was selfish because it wasn't just me I was putting in danger, and the truth is I'm horrified at myself that I tried. But every single day I woke up, I'd puke until dinner. My parents would force me to eat something, and then I'd throw that up before bed.

I was miserable, hungry, tired, and living the surreal experience of my parents selling their condo to move into the home where I intended to raise a family with you. My whole life felt like it was launching backwards against a steamroller barrelling impenetrably forward. That steamroller was the size of an egg and siphoning every nutrient from any morsel of food I could consume.

I read baby books, and couldn't relate to the smiling mothers cooing at their cheery babes in the photos. Nothing I read made me feel prepared for what was coming. You weren't here to tell me, 'It's fine, Linds. You're overthinking again, but you know nothing ever turns out as bad as you imagine it will.'

The night you died was the first time you were wrong about that.

Money was tight even with the money for my parents' condo, because your salary paid the mortgage and mine paid half of the rest of our bills. I always knew how much more you made. I just had no concept of what living in the world without it would actually cost.

It was all of these things that drove me to it. And I regret it. I don't want to die. I know that now. Figured it out in the hospital after my dad found me on the bathroom floor. They kept me there for two months. Same hospital in which you died, three floors up.

~ ~ ~

I see my therapist three times a week now. She helps me. We talk about you. She says it's good I can find time to talk to you. She warns me not to talk about you like you're still here, but I see you everywhere. You look at me with that tilted grin, just like you are now. If your parents saw you sitting on the top of your grave like that, they'd flip!

I know I haven't said this to you since the morning before the accident, but I know it's true. I love you. I will always love you, and our kid, who I think I'll love even more than I loved you. I forgive you, and I forgive Jennifer, and I might forgive myself eventually, too.

I don't know if you'll disappear, so tonight, can we just watch the sunset over the mountains. It's such a perfect evening, and I want to remember it like this.

CONTRIBUTORS

Eloise Archer is an Australian poet, writer, author, and creator of the fictional podcast, *This Is Cheaper Than Therapy*. Archer's work ranges from comedic self-help, as is the case in the paperback *How To Be An Adult*, to poetry and speculative fiction. While these genres differ, Archer's themes of the past and its relationship with the future remain constant throughout. Though their work features a range of diverse characters, the unifying threads of loneliness, introspection, and unforgiving humanity are always present. Archer's poetry has been published on Honey & Lime Literary Magazine's Oceans & Time. They are currently working on a collection of poetry.

For both previous and upcoming projects visit **eloisearcher.wixsite.com/site** or follow Eloise on Twitter at **@_EloiseArcher** and on Instagram at **@_eloisearcher**.

Ioanna Arka was born and raised in Athens, Greece. She studied Physics at the University of Athens and has a doctorate degree in Theoretical Astrophysics from the University of Heidelberg, Germany. She has worked as a researcher in Astrophysics and Climate Science. She has published popular science articles on blogs and scientific articles in peer-reviewed journals.

Ioanna is a self-proclaimed linguistics nerd who harbors a deep love of the English language and a passion for literature. Starting from High Fantasy as a teenager, she veered into Horror, Thrillers, Non-fiction, Literary fiction, and Classics.

Today, Ioanna works as a freelance beta reader, proofreader, and literary editor. She lives in Germany with her husband and their two children. She is an avid cook and baker. Her husband and children and all their neighbors are very happy for all the Greek food and the delicious cakes she prepares on a daily basis.

Emma Deshpande is a writer pursuing an MFA from New York University. She grew up in Mystic, Connecticut, and attended high school in New Haven. She moved to London, England for university when she was eighteen, and lived there for four years before moving back to America. Her short stories *Iphis Without a God* and *Breakfast* appeared in the 2017 and 2018 University College London Publisher's Prize Anthologies, respectively. *Breakfast* also won the anthology's first place prize in 2018. Her short story *They Could Be Anywhere* was shortlisted for the 53rd Jerry Jazz Musician Short Fiction Contest. She is half Indian and half Irish, and she wants to increase representation of biracial families. She is currently editing a novel manuscript about young Indian-Irish and Indian-American people living in New Haven. For a few years, all her stories were set in hospitals and nursing homes. Three of her grandparents suffered from degenerative diseases, and she wanted to give them voices after they stopped being able to communicate themselves. When she can't work with words, she sews; she enjoys embroidering and sewing clothes by hand. Her book reviews and blog are at **deshpandewrites.com** and on Instagram at **@deshpande_writes**.

Zev Good grew up between East Tennessee and Alabama, and has lived his entire life in the South. His first published work of fiction was the story collection *A Map of the World*, from 2017. His debut novel, *All About the Benjamins*, was published in 2019. He lives in a suburb of Atlanta with his husband and two dogs the size of ponies, and is at work on his next novel.

R. Tim Morris has self-published four novels of literary fiction (*Molt*, *The Inevitable Fall of Tommy Mueller*, *This Never Happened*, and *To Be Honest*). He is currently working on his fifth, this one a dark fairy tale/fantasy entitled *The Lost Memories of Oceans*. In all of them, Morris thrives on shaping his stories into intricate puzzles, begging the reader to take a second look. His writing has appeared in the Owl Canyon Press Short Story Hackathon. He lives in Vancouver, British Columbia and works as a library technician. You can find him on Twitter at **@RyMo89** or visit his website at **rtimmorris.com**.

Natalie Pinter developed an appreciation for the dark and fantastical at a young age and has been an accomplished daydreamer for most of her waking life. After spending many years working as a bookseller, she finally started sharing her own stories. Her debut novel, *The Fragile Keepers*, will be published in 2021 by Sunbury Press. You can find her on Twitter at **@cultofpersonat** and on Instagram at **@cultofpersonatalie**.

Justine Rosenberg is the author of *The Metals Trilogy*, a fantasy series in the works. She also dabbles in poetry and literary fiction. Born in California and raised in the Pacific Northwest, she currently resides in Vancouver, British Columbia, with her husband. To find out more about her various writing projects, follow her on Twitter at **@squidinkmoon** or visit her website at **jlimrosenbergwrites.com**.

Chet Sandberg is an independent author from the Upper Peninsula of Michigan who works in the genres of Fantasy, Science Fiction, Literary Drama, Literary Comedy, and LitRPG. He's also a reluctant nurse, working primarily in cardiology step down or progressive care units, as well as a freelance line and style editor for several independent authors. Find him at **chetnovels.com**, on Twitter at **@Chet_Novels**, or join his fan Facebook group called *Chet Sandberg's Close Readers*. He also co-hosts a podcast for writers called *Borderline Genius* with the wonderful Nora McKinney.

Abby Simpson has written fiction for publication in VampCat Magazine, Gestalt Media, and more, but always finds herself wishing she had "more time" to write. A contributing author for DeanBlundell.com, she blogs about topical and social issues from her home in beautiful Vancouver, British Columbia, and is always trying to carve out time for hiking and finishing her first novel's manuscript (though rarely at the same time). Online, you can find her on Twitter at **@abbythetweet**.

Isana Skeete is an ace non-binary immigrant living in Miami, Florida. Their life was changed when they first read *Alice's Adventures in Wonderland* and *Through the Looking-Glass and What Alice Found There*. Ever since then, they have been obsessed with reading what they like to call "profound nonsense."

With degrees in German Studies, Book Conservation and soon Creative Writing and maybe Library Science, they love to learn new things. But their true passion is writing the fantasy and speculative fiction featuring queer characters of colour that wasn't around when they needed it most.

Though they have an aversion to social media for mental health reasons, they can still be found on Instagram at **@iamanelfchild**.

They are currently an MFA student at NYU.

Lior Torenberg is an Israeli-American writer living and working in New York City. She received her Bachelors at Boston College and is in the process of receiving her Masters in Creative Writing from New York University. Her writing centers around the personal and psychological growth of women, with an emphasis on sexuality and family dynamics. Though primarily a novelist, she is known to dabble in the dark arts of poetry and short stories when time permits. She has had pieces published in literary magazines including Stylus and Spilt Milk. When she's not writing, Lior can be found overpaying for coffee and constructing crosswords. She can be reached on Twitter at **@LTorenberg** or on her website at **liortorenberg.wixsite.com/home**.

Perry Wolfecastle is a writer currently living the Staffordshire Moorlands, England. Perry writes both fiction and non-fiction, and although he has a taste for the darker side of fantasy, he has been known to dabble in other genres such as horror and science fiction, as well as experimenting in non-genre fiction.

Holding a bachelor's degree in History from the Open University, Perry can be found posting articles and book reviews over at **perrywolfecastle.com**. The articles he posts range from deep dives into the science behind Mary Shelley's Frankenstein to the Vikings' arrival on the North American continent, and why exactly did Bram Stoker believe Elizabeth I was a man.

His first book, a non-fiction work entitled *How to Start Winning Against Procrastination*, will release in 2020, with his first longer form of fiction (tentatively entitled *Promised Land*) scheduled to be released in early 2021.

You can find Perry talking nonsense on Twitter at **@PWolfecastle**.

Perry has recently discovered that he dislikes talking about himself in the third person.

Lightning Source UK Ltd.
Milton Keynes UK
UKHW010635300920
370791UK00002B/307